PUFFIN BOOKS

THE HYDROFOIL MYSTERY

Eric Walters has written many children's novels including *Trapped in Ice*, which won the Silver Birch Award, was nominated for both the Ruth Schwartz and Geoffrey Bilson awards, and was a Canadian Children's Book Centre Choice. His most recent novel is *The Bully Boys*. He lives in Mississauga with his wife and their three children.

THE
HYDROFOIL
MYSTERY

ERIC WALTERS

Puffin Books

PUFFIN BOOKS

Published by the Penguin Group

Penguin Books Canada Ltd, 10 Alcorn Avenue, Toronto, Ontario, Canada M4V 3B2

Penguin Books Ltd, 27 Wrights Lane, London W8 5TZ, England

Penguin Putnam Inc., 375 Hudson Street, New York, New York 10014, U.S.A.

Penguin Books Australia Ltd, Ringwood, Victoria, Australia

Penguin Books (NZ) Ltd, cnr Rosedale and Airborne Roads, Albany,
Auckland 1310, New Zealand

Penguin Books Ltd, Registered Offices: Harmondsworth, Middlesex, England

First published in Viking by Penguin Books Canada Limited, 1999

Published in Puffin Books, 2000

10 9 8 7 6 5 4

Manufactured in Canada

CANADIAN CATALOGUING IN PUBLICATION DATA

Walters, Eric, 1957–
    The hydrofoil mystery

ISBN 0-14-130220-8

I. Title.

PS8595.A598H92 2000   jC813'.54   C99-932518-3
PZ7.W34Hy 2000

Visit Penguin Canada's web site at **www.penguin.ca**

Alexander Graham Bell was a genius—probably after da Vinci, the greatest thinker of all time. But more than a genius he was a devoted husband, a caring father and a wonderful grandparent. He was a man of integrity, honesty, honour, who still loved a good joke. He himself said his occupation was that of teacher. Thank you Mr. Bell for being both my inspiration and a teacher to me.

Acknowledgements

I would like to thank Mr. Jack Stephens, retired Superintendent of The Alexander Graham Bell Museum in Baddeck, N.S., for helping me to understand the greatness of Alexander Graham Bell.

THE
HYDROFOIL
MYSTERY

Chapter One

June, 1917

THE TRAIN JOLTED SLIGHTLY forward and my eyes were jarred open. I looked around. We weren't going yet; we were still in the station. It was just another car being added to the train before we headed north.

I closed my eyes again. I knew I'd probably drift off. I was so tired... I hadn't slept more than a few minutes all of the previous night. I'd been too upset to go to sleep. Too upset and too angry... at my mother. What right did she have to send me away for the summer? Away from all my friends and everything I knew. About as far away as you could get from Halifax without leaving Nova Scotia entirely.

And the way she sprang it on me. No hint, no warning. She just came to me out of the blue that night and said I was being sent away in the morning to work on some estate up in Baddeck on Cape Breton Island. She told me she hadn't said anything about it before because she hadn't wanted to "get my hopes up." She said she had just received the telegram that night confirming the arrangements. The way she talked, she tried to make it seem like a big adventure. I was going to go up to work for the "famous" Alexander Graham Bell, the inventor of the telephone. She blathered on and on about what an opportunity it was, how many young men from throughout the Maritimes wanted to have this position and how it was only through the influence of an old schoolmate of hers that I had been fortunate enough to be hired. How was it fortunate to be the servant of some rich man and his family? She worked hard to convince me it was going to be exciting.

But I knew the truth. It was excitement she wanted to get me away from. She thought I was running with the wrong crowd. She didn't seem to like any of my friends... at least not my new friends. Thank goodness she didn't know the half of it. After my mother and sister would go to bed at night I'd often sneak out. My friends would be waiting for me at the end of the street. Of course none of *them* had to sneak out. They were all older than me. Tim and John were both nineteen, but I did look a lot older than fifteen and could pass for eighteen ... at least some of the time. That was good, because you had to look older to get into the places we liked to go. Once I even thought about lying about my age and trying to join the army, but the guys told me I should let other people fight the war.

All around Halifax there were places where men met and played cards and tossed dice and drank and smoked. I'd only smoked a couple of times and I didn't drink at all, but I did like being with my friends. They were showing me the ropes. Tim was a pro. He knew cards, and on a good night he could win more money than most dock workers could make in an entire week.

Besides the local men there was always a new supply of soldiers. They came to Halifax by rail and were temporarily stationed there, waiting for a ship to take them across the Atlantic Ocean to fight in the war in Europe. And of course there were always dozens and dozens of sailors present any place there was gambling. My father's a sailor, and he'd told me that gambling to sailors is like honey to a bee…irresistible. With the war on, there was no end of work for the merchant sailors working the Atlantic convoys. They'd barely make port before they'd hook up with another ship and head out again.

At least that's how it was with my father. He'd always been gone more than he was home, but for the past year he'd been gone almost constantly. It really didn't matter much to me anyway—even when he was home he really wasn't. Sometimes I'd get angry about things, but my mother would explain to me and my sister that it was just the life of a sailor. We had to understand that he'd be there more for us if he could, but he had to earn money to support us. So if he was working so much more now, how come money was tighter than ever? It was so tight Mom had to take in laundry. And of course, with her working evenings, that left me to take care of Sarah.

What my mother didn't know—what I couldn't tell

her—was that I knew there were times he was back in Halifax, but didn't even bother to stop in to see us.

One night, one of those times I'd gone out without my mother knowing, I'd been in the basement of the Crown Hotel. There was always a card game going on there, twenty-four hours a day, seven days a week. I was sitting off in a corner watching all the activity. And then I caught sight of him.

At first I couldn't be sure. He was at the far side of the room, and smoke filled the air with a thick haze, but as I looked hard and long I realized there was no mistake. It was my father. He was playing poker, throwing chips on the pile recklessly with one hand while pouring down drinks with the other. Part of me wanted to go up and see him—after all, he'd been gone for over three months —but how would I explain what I was doing there in the middle of the night? Besides, I could see he'd been drinking. I slunk out without being seen and headed home. I figured I'd see him soon enough when he came home in the morning, but he didn't come home. Not the next day, or the next or the next.

A full month passed before we got a letter from him, from Liverpool. There was no mention in that letter of him ever having been back in Halifax. He said he'd been laid up in England and because of that he couldn't send us much money this time—he hoped we could get by for a while longer. In my mind I kept seeing him throwing away money in that card game—money that we needed to survive.

When he finally came home, mother and Sarah were so glad to see him. I didn't even want to be in the same room with him, but I had to pretend I was happy he was there. Later on that night, when mother was putting Sarah to bed, he started asking me questions. He wanted to know what was wrong with me, and wasn't I glad he was home, and why wasn't I treating my old man with respect? I just sat there and took it, not answering, just mumbling or making up excuses—until he put his hands on me and shoved me up against the wall. I swore I'd never let him hit me again. For the first time in my life I pushed back, and I told him about seeing him in the hotel basement and what I thought of him. Then I ran out. I stayed out all night, and when I came back the next day he was gone.

More and more, I was spending time with Tim and the guys. And the more they got to know me, the better we got along. They were now trusting me enough to let me in on what was going on in the games. They weren't just good card players, they were card sharks. Tim knew some tricks—things like dealing off the bottom of the deck, stacking the cards and holding onto cards that he wanted—and he was helping me to learn as well. Whenever I had spare time I'd practise the tricks they'd shown me. And lately I'd started to do much more than just watch the games. I'd become a player, and a good player. Tim said I had "a way" about me and was doing the things they'd shown me even better than they could. Soon it wasn't just them winning money, it was me as well.

Of course, sometimes things got out of hand in those games. Nobody liked to lose money, especially if it didn't seem fair. So far, though, quick legs and quicker minds had got us out of any trouble we'd gotten into. What we couldn't talk our way out of we'd been able to run away from. Well, all except for the one time the police brought me home at two in the morning.

I can still see the look of shock and disappointment on my mother's face when she opened that door and saw me standing with the officer. He explained how I'd been a "found-in" when they raided a gambling house. She hardly spoke a word to me that night or the next morning. I wished she would yell. It would have been easier.

The train jolted again and my eyes popped open. I instantly realized that we weren't just adding another car, the train was starting to move out of the station. A number of passengers were leaning out of the windows, waving goodbye to friends or family on the platform. I knew my mother would be standing there, looking for me. Part of me wanted to go and wave to her—it was the last I was going to see of her for at least two months—but I remained slumped in my seat. I hadn't hugged her back when she had wrapped her arms around me before I boarded the train, or answered her when she'd said "I love you." Maybe she could send me away, but she couldn't make me say goodbye.

"Wake up, son."

I looked up to see the conductor standing over top of me.

"I need to see your ticket."

Half asleep, I fumbled in my jacket pocket, pulled it out and handed it to him.

"Going all the way to Iona, I see," he said.

"No," I answered, shaking my head. "Baddeck. I'm heading to Baddeck."

"You may be, but this train isn't. Iona is the end of the line."

"But how can I get to Baddeck?" I asked anxiously.

"There's a ferry out of Iona that goes across Bras d'Or Lake, it'll get you there," he said as he punched my ticket and then handed it back to me. He started to walk away.

"How far are we out of Halifax?" I called after him.

He turned back to face me. "Almost five hours."

I had no idea I'd been asleep that long. I'd drifted off a few more times after we'd left Halifax, but it seemed every few minutes the train stopped at some little station in the middle of nowhere to pick up or drop off passengers and parcels. I guess at some point I really had fallen asleep. The only question now was how I was going to spend the remaining ten hours of this trip. I got up. I needed to find a washroom and stretch my legs.

I left my bags there at the seat and started down the aisle toward the rear of the train. More than half of the seats were empty. The occupied ones were filled with a variety of different people—men, probably farmers, dressed in overalls and sitting by themselves, whole families with children sleeping between their parents, and salesmen in stiff-collared suits with their sample cases at their feet. I pushed open the door and stepped out between the two cars. Up above, in the gap of open sky, was a stream of black smoke flowing back from the engine. As I stood there, a few flecks of soot and ash dropped down onto my face. I brushed them away and moved into the adjoining club car.

I had no sooner stepped inside than I spied a card game going on. Four tired-looking salesmen were sitting facing each other around a table. Their sample cases were pushed out into the aisle. I slowed down as I got close to them. They were laughing loudly, and I saw one of them take a long swig from a flask and pass the bottle to the guy beside him. He took a drink and coughed loudly. Whatever was in that flask must have been strong stuff. As I passed by I saw a stack of bills and coins in front of each man, as well as a pile of money in the middle. I also noticed that each man was holding five cards. They were playing straight poker—one of my favourite games. Casually, I passed just beyond the game and took a seat on the edge of a chair just two down from them. I figured I'd found the way to pass the remaining hours on the train.

"Well kid, how many cards do you want?" the dealer asked gruffly.

"Two cards," I answered, discarding the two I didn't want face down into the pile. Awkwardly, he dealt me two cards to replace them. After watching the original card players for the better part of an hour I'd worked up the nerve to ask to play. At first they'd been reluctant, but when they'd found out I had money, and no parent on board the train to look after me, they'd agreed to deal me in. Over the next few hours I'd played poker and managed to more than double my money. Instead of just the five dollars my mother had given me, and twelve dollars she didn't even know I had, I was now sitting on almost thirty-five bucks.

There was a steady stream of new players as one salesman reached his destination and left the train to be replaced in the game by somebody who'd just come on board. Nobody was there long enough to win or lose more than a few dollars. For the most part they weren't bad players. The way these old guys all seemed to know each other, I suspected that travelling salemen played cards almost as much as sailors.

The next hand was dealt. As I looked at my cards I tried to mentally count the money sitting in my pile. There was still a long way to go, and if I could keep on winning at this pace I'd have over a hundred dollars in my pocket before we reached Iona. Maybe that would be enough for me to just turn back around—buy a ticket back to Halifax, spend the summer with my friends and forget all about being some fancy servant in Baddeck. Boy, would that be something.

"How about if we raise the limit on bets?" I said.

The other three men looked up from their cards and directly at me, and the guy dealing stopped for a minute.

"What did you have in mind, kid?" the dealer asked.

"I don't know. Maybe we could double it," I suggested. Nobody spoke. "Unless you gentleman aren't up to the challenge," I added, not so subtly taunting them.

"Hah! I think I can handle that action," one of them responded.

"Unless your mama's going to object," added another, and they all started to chuckle.

"My mother is two hundred miles down the line from here. You sure your mamas and wives are okay with it?"

The dealer looked around at the other players. One scowled and the other three smiled slightly, but all nodded in agreement. "Okay, kid, I think we might be prepared to take some of your money… after all, it's as good as anybody else's. Let's play poker."

Chapter Two

"SON, ARE YOU ALL right?" the conductor asked.

"I'm fine," I said softly, lifting my head off my hands.

"It's just that we've been in the station a while. Everybody else has already disembarked. This is the end of the line. You are getting off, aren't you?"

I nodded my head. What choice did I have now? Slowly I rose and then bent down to pick up my two bags.

"Did you lose much money?" he asked.

"A little," I answered. What I couldn't answer—what I could hardly believe—was that I'd lost everything. In my pocket were the few coins I had left. Somewhere down the line things had started to go wrong. At first it happened slowly, but then it got worse and worse. And as I started to lose I got more desperate to try to win back what I'd lost and try to gain what I needed to escape from a summer in Baddeck. But it didn't work. I'd never seen such luck before! Hand after hand, they just kept on winning and I kept on losing. Finally, in one drastic bid to get even all at once, I bet almost all that I had left... and lost. It was right after that that the four salesmen all said they'd reached their station and left the train together.

"I've seen those men play poker before. They don't seem to lose too often," the conductor said. "I figure a few of them make more money off the gaming table than they do selling anything out of their sample cases." He paused. "You're going to Baddeck, aren't you?"

I nodded.

"Then you really better get moving. The *Blue Hill* is scheduled to be leaving soon."

"The *Blue Hill*?"

"The ferry that goes to Baddeck." He pulled out his watch. "She leaves in about five min—"

His words were drowned out by the blast of a loud horn.

"That would be the *Blue Hill* letting everybody know she's almost built up a big enough head of steam to be heading out," he continued.

"Where do I find the ship?" I asked in alarm as I stumbled down the aisle after the conductor.

He stopped and held the door to the next car. "She better be in the lake or there'll be trouble," he laughed. He saw I wasn't enjoying his little joke and his expression and tone changed. "Just go down the street to the town wharf. The *Blue Hill* will be tied.. ."

His words were again lost in the blast of its horn.

"And you better hurry, son. If you miss her, she won't be back until tomorrow morning."

"Tomorrow! How do I get to the ship?" I asked in panic.

He raised his hand and pointed out the window. "Foot of the street. You can't miss her. She's the biggest thing at the wharf."

I grabbed my bag and flung it on my shoulder. I bumped past the conductor still holding the door and bounded down the stairs of the carriage two at a time. I hit the ground running, and almost tumbled over. A wide, dirt street ran downhill from the station. It was lined on both sides with stores and plank sidewalks. Horses and carriages were tied up at the hitching posts. At the bottom of the street, no more than two or three blocks away, I could see the shimmer of water. The ship's horn blared again and I doubled my pace. Ever since hearing that I'd be spending my summer working in Baddeck, I'd thought it was the last place on earth I wanted to be. Now I realized it was the second-last place; the last would be stranded here for the night.

Hitting the foot of the street I saw the wharf just over to the side. A number of vessels, including a large ship I hoped was the *Blue Hill*, were still at the dock. There was smoke rising from its stack, and a couple of sailors were by the lines getting ready to cast off.

"Wait!" I yelled.

A woman and a young girl up ahead turned and stared at me, but neither of the sailors even looked up from their work. My voice couldn't carry over the sounds of the ship's engine. One of the men threw his line aboard the vessel and jumped on after it. I hit the wharf and the pounding of my feet echoed against the wood. The second man stood up and tossed his line onto the ship, which slowly started into motion, gliding parallel to the dock. It was moving, but I was gaining.

"Hold on! Wait!"

Both sailors, one on the dock and the second on the ship, looked up at me, but they were helpless now to stop the boat. It was picking up speed, and a little slit of water opened between it and the dock. It was only a few feet away; I was going to miss it by a few crummy feet... or was I?

"AAAAAHHHH!" I screamed as I reached the edge of the dock and leaped into the air, hitting the deck of the ship and rolling forward, until I crashed into a bulkhead.

"Jeeze! Are ya crazy, laddie?"

I looked up at the sailor who'd cast off the lines. He was old and grizzled. A second sailor, not that much older than me, rushed over, and the two of them pulled me to my feet. I bent down and picked up my bag.

"I... I... had to... catch... the ferry," I panted, trying to get my breath.

"You almost caught yourself a dip in the lake. Where are you going that's so all-fired important you couldn't wait for tomorrow's ferry?" the older sailor asked.

"Baddeck. I'm... going to... Baddeck." A terrible thought flooded my mind. What if this wasn't the *Blue Hill*? What if I'd jumped onto the wrong ferry? In my headlong rush I hadn't time to even look around to see if this was the right ship.

"The *Blue Hill*... this is the *Blue Hill*? Right?"

The sailors exchanged a look and they both started to chuckle.

"Be mighty funny if you went to all this effort and jumped onto the wrong ship, wouldn't it?" the older sailor asked.

"The wrong ship... you mean this is the wrong ship?" I questioned in a trembling voice.

"Herbie, don't be giving the kid such a hard time," the younger man cautioned.

"I'm just playing with the lad. This is the *Blue Hill*. It would be mighty funny *if* you'd jumped on the wrong ship, is all."

"We're Baddeck bound. What's so important about you getting there?" the younger man asked.

"I'm going up there to work for the summer." I deliberately didn't tell them where. I didn't want anybody to think of me as some sort of servant or farm hand.

"Well, you'll get there in time for work tomorrow. Now, judging by the way you came aboard, I would guess you didn't have time to pay your fare."

"No... I didn't have time."

"Well you have time now. We won't be getting into Baddeck for close to four hours. You just go and see the first mate and pay for your passage."

I pushed my left hand deep into the pocket of my trousers and felt for the few remaining coins. There were four or five. "How much is it?" I asked, wondering if I had enough and what would happen if I didn't. I pictured myself shovelling coal into the boiler for the entire trip.

"Twenty-five cents for a one-way trip. And if you're looking for a little breakfast you can find fresh buns, baked goods and hot coffee in the forward lounge. We always put aboard the best fresh baking from the bakery in Iona."

I dug the coins out and looked at them. Two dimes, a nickel and a penny. Enough for the passage but not for breakfast.

"I'm not really hungry," I lied.

Almost on cue my stomach gurgled, and I felt like cursing out loud.

"Come on with me and we'll find the first mate," Herbie said as he started around the side of the ship. I fell in behind. We circled around to the front and he pointed out a man with a beard standing at the very prow of the ship.

I started toward the first mate.

"Hold on, son," Herbie called out, and I stopped. "The mate might be a little bit miffed about you coming on without a ticket... especially if he hears how you came aboard. Give me your money and I'll take care of things for you."

Was he trying to get my money? Was he tricking me? I tightened the hold on my cash.

"Come on, lad, do you think I'm trying to take your few coins?" Herbie asked.

"No," I lied uncomfortably. Hesitantly I turned over the money. I watched him walk over to the other sailor. I felt better when I saw them exchange a few words I couldn't hear, then Herbie pointed in my direction and pressed the coins into the other man's hand.

I looked away and around the ship. It was fairly large for a ferry. Other sailors were working on the deck, and a

few passengers milled around or stood at the railing looking out at the water. It was calm, and except for the wake
of the ferry there was hardly a ripple on the surface. The
sun was bright and there weren't any clouds anywhere in
the sky. What little breeze there was carried the smell of
the baked goods from the lounge. I inhaled deeply and
my stomach rumbled in response.

"Here you go, laddie."

I turned around. It was Herbie, and he was holding
out a cup of steaming coffee and a bun split down the
middle with orange marmalade peeking out.

"Take these," he said.

"I'm not hungry," I immediately replied.

"First thing, you are hungry. Second, even if you
weren't you'd still want to sink your teeth into this bun.
Now take them!" he ordered. "And don't worry none
about the money."

My eyes fell to my feet.

"No crime in being a little short. I've been there a few
times myself. If it makes it any easier, think of it as a
loan."

"A loan?"

"Yep. Baddeck is a small place. We'll run into each
other a few times during the summer. You pay me back
by buying me a coffee. Okay?"

"Thanks," I said as I reached out and took the offer-
ings. The bun was still warm and I took a big bite. It was
delicious! A little dribble of warm marmalade escaped
from the corner of my mouth and started to run down
toward my chin. I flicked out my tongue and captured it
before it could get away.

"Where are you going to be working?" Herbie asked.

"At the Bell place," I answered reluctantly.

"Then you'll surely have the money to pay me back. No matter what people may say about old man Bell, nobody ever questioned his money. He pays good and he pays on time."

"What do people say about Bell?" I asked. I wondered if he had a reputation for being nasty with his hired hands and that's why he had to get help from so far away, because none of the locals would work for him.

"Some people say he's a bit batty."

"Batty?" I asked.

"You know... a little touched," Herbie replied, tapping a finger against the side of his head.

"What do you mean?"

"Man is reported to spend most of his nights walking around the back roads of the county. Just wandering, sometimes muttering to his self or laughing out loud. Doesn't even have the sense to come inside when it starts to rain—just keeps walking. And you hear about all manner of peculiarities up at that estate." He paused. "Building and flying gigantic kites, and experiments with sheep and... but I shouldn't be spreading rumours about things I don't know."

What I wanted him to do was spread more than a little bit of the rumours. Or maybe I wished he'd said nothing at all. Even I knew a little bit about Alexander Graham Bell. The telephone was just one of his inventions. The way I'd heard it, there was nothing he wouldn't experiment with if it took his fancy. He'd even done some work on steam-powered aircraft.

"But you know it's just like they say," Herbie explained, "genius and insanity are opposite sides of the same coin, and the man is a genius... even if he is batty."

I turned to face out over the railing onto the lake. What had my mother gotten me into? She had arranged for the job through an old grade school friend, Mrs. McCauley-Brown, who was the head of Bell's household staff. Maybe I should have argued more with her, maybe I should have just refused to go. Then again, knowing my mother, she might have tried to put me over her shoulder and carry me to the train. I was certainly much bigger than her, but nobody was more determined. She was probably the most stubborn person I'd ever met. More than once she'd told me that saying somebody was a stubborn Scotsman was like saying the same thing twice.

I couldn't help but wonder if things might have been different if my father had been around more. He probably wouldn't have made me go. But then again, if he were at home I probably would have wanted to leave.

"My name's Herbert Campbell. My friends call me Herbie. What's your name, son?"

"Billy McCracken."

"Pleased to meet you, Billy," he said, thrusting out his hand.

I popped the last of my bun into my mouth and shook his hand.

"This is a nice ship. What is it, about a hundred and twenty feet in length?"

"Yeah, almost exactly. One hundred and twenty-three," Herbie answered.

"What does she displace?"

"About 350 tons, empty, and up to 420 fully loaded."

"Must be a shallow keel. How many feet of water does she need under her?"

"Under five feet," Herbie said. "Where'd you learn about ships, Billy?"

"My father."

"He's a sailor is he?"

"Merchant marine. Cargo ships mostly . . . Atlantic crossings."

"That's real sailing, not like this little delivery boat. This is nothing but a glorified grocery boat!" Herbie exclaimed. "And of course, except for that one lad you met when you came on board, this ship is all crewed by old men. The younger sailors are all working on the Atlantic crossing, or at war. I worked the North Atlantic myself for over thirty years. Had two ships go down underneath me and lived to tell of it.

"In those days, of course, I only had to worry about wind, waves and ice. Now with the war those ships have to be dodging German submarines... there's been a terrible toll taken... I hear that more than four hundred ships went down in April alone, around 875,000 tons to the bottom of the..." Herbie stopped and looked up at me. "I'm sorry. I shouldn't be talking to you about such things, what with your father and all."

"That's all right," I said softly. It wasn't like he was telling me something that I didn't know. I read the shipping reports in the newspapers listing the names of the ships that had been sunk. Since my father was crewing on so many different ships, we didn't even know the name of the ship he was on most of the time. The only way we'd ever find out if he was lost was if we received a visit from the government man—going from house to house to tell a woman and her children that their man's ship had gone down.

The only thing worse than him coming to our door would be if it happened when I couldn't be there with my mother. No matter what I knew, she still loved him.

Chapter Three

I SPENT THE REST OF the voyage standing at the railing, staring out over the water. We never seemed to stray very far from land, and the ship put in at three small towns before I overheard another passenger say that Baddeck was on the horizon.

The first things to appear were the tall, thin spires of two churches. Next I could start to make out the outlines of buildings. Everything seemed to be painted a bright white and stood out against the dark greens and browns of the surrounding country-side. As we cruised in toward the town wharf, I could see a series of smaller wooden buildings, prob-ably stores and houses, as well as a number of larger stone and brick structures. Then, well away from the village, my eye was caught by the sight of a large building, high on a hill, set back from the water's edge. There were all sorts of peaks and sections to the place, and while I couldn't be sure, I thought this must be the Bell mansion.

With a slight bump, the *Blue Hill* touched in at the wharf. I circled around to the front of the vessel, where I'd set down my bag. The sailors were busy tying off the ship while the passengers were gathering their possessions and lining up to leave as soon as the gangplank was set into place. I fell in behind the others and the line soon began moving. I stepped off the ship and began walking down the wharf toward the town.

"Hey, Billy!" a voice called out behind me.

I turned around. It was Herbie.

"I'll be seeing you around town. Don't be forgetting about my coffee!"

I smiled, and waved.

He smiled back and returned to making the bow fast to the wharf.

It was obvious Baddeck wasn't a big place, but it certainly was active. People, many of the men dressed in fancy waistcoats and the women wearing their Sunday-best dresses and big fancy hats, milled along the plank walkways that lined the wide dirt street. A number of horses and wagons were tied up or moving slowly up the road. I wondered if there was something special going on in town, and then I remembered it was Sunday, and these people had probably just left one of the big churches whose spires were so visible from out on the water. Mother and Sarah were probably just leaving church now. I didn't know where my father was—at sea or in port—but I did know he wasn't in church.

There were also two buildings, a hotel and a court-house, which loomed larger than the surrounding stores. The courthouse wasn't of any interest to me, but I'd never heard of a hotel that wasn't home to an occasional card or dice game.

"You look lost, son."

I looked over. A policeman stood in front of me, in a polished uniform.

"Nope, I'm not lost."

"Did you come in on the morning ferry?" he asked. He had a distinctive Irish accent.

"Yes, I did," I answered in surprise. How did he know?

"Don't look so shocked. It's my job to keep track of the comings and goings of everybody, and you're one of only a few strangers on this whole street. What's your name and business in Baddeck?"

"I'm going to be working at the Bell mansion," I answered, giving him only part of what he'd requested.

"It's called Beinn Bhreagh."

"Beinn what?" I asked.

"Beinn Bhreagh. It's Gaelic for 'beautiful mountain.' That's the name Mr. and Mrs. Bell gave to their place when they first came to Baddeck."

"Is it that big place up on the hill?"

"Yes, it is. You probably saw it from the ferry. Best way to get there is to walk along the main road out of town to the east. It'll take you less than twenty minutes . . . fifteen, if you walk with determination."

"Thanks. I better get going," I said and turned to walk away.

"Hold on a second," the officer instructed, and I stopped in my tracks.

"My name is Corporal O'Malley, and you were forgetting to tell me your name."

"Um… Billy McCracken."

"Well, Mr. McCracken, it was a pleasure to meet you, and I'm sure I'll be seeing you around town occasionally. After all, there's nothing that goes on in these parts that I'm not aware of. Nothing. Good day to you," he said, and he spun on his heel and marched off down the street, the soles of his boots clicking against the plank sidewalk.

This certainly didn't seem like the "friendly" country reception I'd expected. I stepped down off the crowded walk and onto the street, starting off in the opposite direction.

I entered the property through an arched gate in a low stone wall that stretched out in both directions and curved out of sight. The house was set well back from the road, and the driveway was long and better maintained than the road running by the estate. The house was gigantic, and the closer I got the larger it seemed to become. The lower levels were constructed of fieldstone, topped by green clapboard for two storeys, then covered by a dark brown roof. The roof was broken up by a few dormer windows and six different sets of chimneys poking up into the sky. The windows and trim were painted white, and a large deck and a glass-enclosed sunroom stretched most of the way across the front of the house. Off to the side stood two flagpoles; at the top of one fluttered the "Stars and Stripes," while a Union Jack adorned the second. Farther back I could see a number of other buildings; at least two of them looked even bigger than the house. I wondered what they were for. A few people were moving in the distance. Cautiously I approached the house.

I walked along the verandah and stopped in front of a large door. I took a deep breath, reached out and pushed the doorbell. A harsh ringing came from within the house. Almost immediately I heard the sound of rushing footsteps and the door was flung open. A young woman in an apron stood before me.

"Yes?" she asked.

"I'm here to see Mrs. McCauley-Brown."

"Are you now? And does she know you're coming?"

"Yes, she does, but she didn't know I was coming today exactly… just sometime this week, I think."

"I see. Step in and I'll get her," the woman said, holding the door open wide.

As soon as I stepped in she closed the door behind me and rushed off. I looked around the entranceway. There was a large stone fireplace off to the side and another wall was covered by shelves crammed with books. The carpeting was fancy and the ceiling extended high above my head.

"Ahh, you must be Billy!" a plump, motherly woman called out as she rushed into the room and wrapped her arms around me, hugging me tightly. She released her grip and took a step back, still holding me by the shoulders. "And you look so much like your mother! You have Cora's eyes and nose for sure you do, for sure!"

"I guess… I mean… here," I said, pulling a letter out of my pocket. "This is from my mother."

"Wonderful! Bless her heart. Now come with me and I'll have a chance to read it." She opened the front door and motioned for me to go back outside. I felt confused but followed her direction. She led me along the porch, down a set of steps and around to the side of the house. "That's the main entrance, Billy, and it's just for guests of the Bells'. You shan't be using that any more. When you come up to the main house, you need to be coming in through this door."

Of course, I thought, servants always use the back door so they don't mix with the fancy folks.

We went through the door and into the kitchen. There was a fire in the corner hearth and two young women were bustling around, working at the counters that rimmed the room.

"Please, have a seat. It's not usually this busy around here but we're readying for a gathering tonight. Have you had breakfast?" Mrs. McCauley-Brown asked.

"A bite on the boat."

"A bite isn't nearly enough for a lad as big as you. Hildy, put on a few eggs and a big helping of porridge for Billy."

"Yes, ma'am," one of the women responded immediately. She wasn't much older than me. She gave me a shy smile and returned to her work.

Mrs. McCauley-Brown took a seat beside me and started to open the letter when the door opened and a harried-looking woman burst into the room.

"We have problems, big problems!" the woman stated emphatically.

"What could possibly be that big a problem? No one here is dying," Mrs. McCauley-Brown retorted.

"It's the lobster."

"What about the lobster?" Mrs. McCauley-Brown asked calmly.

"There isn't any. There's none."

"What do you mean none! How can there be no lobster? This is Cape Breton Island, we're surrounded by the ocean, and the ocean is filled with lobster!" She no longer sounded calm.

"It's the fisherman. He said his boats have never come back so empty. He can't meet the order for the party tonight."

"He must! A dinner party at Beinn Bhreagh without lobster is not a possibility!" she said as she bounded to her feet. "I've got to get to town immediately! Immediately!"

She was almost through the door when she skidded to a stop. "Oh my gosh, I almost forgot about you, Billy. Hildy, as soon as he finishes up his breakfast I want you to have someone bring him up to the staff house and get him properly introduced." Then she rushed out the door accompanied by the messenger, closing it noisily behind her.

"It's only like this when there's a party or gathering," Hildy said.

"It seems like there's special guests or a party every other day!" the other woman added. She was kneading dough for bread, and her arms, right to the elbows, were dusted with flour.

"It is busier of late, no denying that," Hildy agreed.

"How many eggs would you be having, and how would you be liking them?"

"Three… or four would be good, and any way would be fine with me," I answered. "And porridge as well, please."

"Definitely there'll be porridge. Mr. Bell insists on porridge every morning," Hildy said. She walked over to the stove with a bowl and started serving porridge out of a large pot. "I think there are more gatherings this year for a reason," she added.

The other woman stopped working and turned to face her.

"It's because of the grandchildren," Hildy explained.

"The grandchildren! How can all these parties be for the grandchildren when they aren't even here?" the baker asked.

Hildy just smiled as she set a heaping bowl of porridge and a spoon on the table in front of me.

The baker thought for a moment, then smiled. "Of course she's right! Mrs. Bell has arranged all these extra gatherings to get her husband's mind off the grandchildren not being here."

"As long as I've been working here there's been at least one of the grandchildren up here for the summer. The Bells just dote on their grandchildren, and this summer none of them will be up here until much later in the season," Hildy said.

"It's unfortunate for Billy, as well," said the baker. "If some of the grandchildren had been coming he would have had somebody to chum about with."

I nearly rolled my eyes. Even if they would let one of

their grandchildren "chum" with a servant, who's to say I wanted to be around them?

"Possibly, but they're a bit younger than him. The eldest wouldn't be any older than fifteen," Hildy replied.

"I'm fifteen," I said through a mouthful of porridge.

"Fifteen! I was taking you for much older... at least sixteen or seventeen!" Hildy exclaimed. "You're a big lad for your age."

Her response didn't surprise me, although it did please me. I was always being mistaken for older. My mother said this was half the reason for the problems I'd got into over the past year, and my father—well, my father didn't know, or care, about any of it.

I followed Hildy out of the kitchen and we circled around to the back of the house.

"Now I want you to wait right here. There's too much happening in the kitchen for you to wait in there. I'll fetch somebody to bring you up to the staff house and get you settled in," Hildy said. "I've got to get back to the kitchen and into my work."

I nodded.

Instead of rushing back, Hildy stood there staring at me. I felt uncomfortable.

"Well?" she asked.

"Well, what?"

"Aren't you forgetting something?"

I looked down. I had my bag. "I don't think so."

"It's apparent you forgot something... your manners... or don't they say thank you when somebody makes you breakfast where you come from?"

"Yeah, I guess I forgot... thanks," I muttered.

"Oh, don't mention it," she smiled. "That was nothing at all. It does me a world of good to feed a lad with such a fine appetite. It's a good thing the Bells are wealthy people, though, or they couldn't afford to feed you for the summer." She chuckled to herself as she walked away and disappeared around the side of the house.

I looked around. I could now see more clearly the buildings that I'd first spied as I walked up the driveway, as well as many others. There were at least a dozen structures, some not much larger than a big shed and others that looked like warehouses. All the buildings were connected by gravel pathways which stood out reddish-brown against the lush green grass that covered everything else. Along the back of the house and running out in a big U shape was a flower bed filled with a dazzling variety of different shaped and coloured flowers.

As my gaze ran along the length of the garden I was startled by the sight of an old man crouched in among the flowers, staring at me. He was dressed in dirty old work clothing and had a thick white beard and a mass of hair that flowed in a thousand different directions. He held a hoe in one hand and some weeds in the other. He motioned for me to come to him. I hesitated, but his gesturing became more animated until I started moving. I stopped when I was standing over top of him.

"What do you think?" he asked.

"Think? About what?"

"The flowers. What do you think about the flowers, the way they're arranged?"

"I don't know anything about flowers," I answered.

"I didn't ask about your horticultural knowledge, I asked what you thought. Even when you don't have any knowledge you still have an opinion. What do you think of the way I've planted them... the way they're arranged?"

"They're all right, I guess."

"Do you think there are too many of the purple flowers?" he asked.

I looked along the length of the bed. "There is a lot of purple," I admitted.

He looked disappointed.

"But I like 'em. They're pretty," I added. "What are they called?"

His face instantly brightened. "They're a type of petunia. They're my favourite. Every year when I plant the flower beds I sneak in a few more of them. There were none here when I first started."

Now I looked at the garden more carefully. There were hundreds of petunias. He must have been here a long time. "How long ago did you start?"

"It's coming up to almost thirty years."

"Thirty years! You've been a gardener here for a long time," I exclaimed.

"It is a long time, but I do a little bit more than just the gardening."

"I guess you must think this is a pretty good place to work."

"Best place in the world as far as I'm concerned. No place else I'd rather be. Can you lend me a hand getting up?" he asked, reaching out an arm.

I grabbed his hand. He was surprisingly solid and I strained to pull him to his feet.

"The legs get a little stiff when I've been weeding too long," he admitted. "So, have you come here to work for the summer?"

"If I can make it through."

He gave me a puzzled look, the lines on his forehead furrowing into deep grooves.

"It's just . . . it wasn't my idea to come up here. I wanted to stay at home."

"And where is home?"

"Halifax. I live with my mother and sister . . . and my father."

"I can understand. It's hard to leave your family behind—"

"And my friends," I interrupted.

"And your friends."

"And besides, I heard that Mr. Bell is a little . . ." I stopped. It probably wasn't wise to be saying any of this since he must know Bell pretty well after having worked here all those years. If I wasn't careful, I could end up getting fired before I'd even started my job. Then, in a flash, I realized that if I did get fired I could simply go back home . . . or wherever else I decided to go instead.

"Heard that Mr. Bell is a little what?" he asked.

"Batty."

"Batty? What on earth does that mean?" he wondered.

"You know, a little bit round the bend, sort of touched."

"Ah, touched! You mean like some kind of a nut!" He laughed.

"Yes, I guess that's what they mean."

"How interesting, how very interesting," he said, shaking his head and continuing to laugh softly to himself.

"And what about you? Do you think he's, what was that word you used, 'batty'?"

"I've never met the man," I admitted.

"You show wisdom in suspending judgment until you've met him, although I know for a fact many of the things he does seem peculiar to many folks."

"You must know him pretty well after all these years."

"Indeed I do, although I must admit, as the years pass I seem to learn some new things and at the same time discover many of the old ideas were incorrect. And what is your name, laddie?"

"Billy, Billy McCracken."

"Billy is a fine name . . . for a goat. I shall call you William. That is your given name, is it not?"

"Yeah, but nobody but my mother and my . . . nobody but my mother calls me that."

"Well, there shall now be another who addresses you by your formal name."

I shrugged. "What's your name?"

"I'm sorry, William, how impolite of me. I'm called many things too, but since I'm addressing you by your first name I suggest you should call me by my given name, Alexander. If you feel that's too forward, I can address you as Mr. McCracken and you may refer to me by my surname . . . Mr. Bell."

Chapter Four

MY HEART SKIPPED A few beats and I swallowed hard to make it start ticking again. Mr. Bell climbed completely out of the flower bed. His laughter became deeper and louder as he walked away toward the big house. I watched him go, and I could still hear him chuckling as he reached the door. He turned around with a big grin on his face, waved and entered the house.

It seemed pretty clear to me that some of the things I'd heard about him were at least halfway true; he did strike me as an odd old bird. I wondered whether I'd really offended him, and if he was even now making arrangements to send me home. It wouldn't be the worst thing, I decided, although having to cable my mother, and then have her send me money for the fare, wouldn't be pleasant.

Especially having to lie to her about what happened to the five dollars she'd given me.

My thoughts were interrupted when I caught sight of a man moving quickly toward me.

"Are you McCracken?" he asked.

"Yes."

"I'm Mr. McGregor. I'm the foreman. Come this way," he said, as he spun on his heels and started walking quickly away.

He was an older man, short and bandy-legged, but I had to move pretty fast to keep up with him. I hurried and fell in step beside him. "Where are we going?"

"Staff house. You've been assigned a room. You'll leave your bag there and I'll give you a tour of the grounds. Let you see what sorts of things go on here."

"Does everybody who works here live at the staff house?" I questioned.

"No, only a few of the employees. Most live in the area and return to their homes in the evening. Nearly all of us live in Baddeck. It's only those 'guests' from the outside who live in the staff house."

"Guests?"

"That's just what the Bells call us. We're all employees, paid by the Bells, but they don't treat us like we're just workers."

"Huh?"

"You'll find it pretty darn interesting to work around here. Hardly ever a dull moment, and if you do your job, and work hard, you'll be treated better than fair. The Bells are good people. Treat everybody mighty fine."

"Can you tell me what I'll be doing?"

"Everything."

"What do you mean everything?" I asked with dread.

"You'll try your hand at near every job on the estate. Mr. Bell likes new people, especially the young ones, to sample everything that's going on."

"I guess he wants to see what people are good at," I suggested.

"That's part of it. The other part is that he considers this to be more than a job. It's part of your education. You'll have a chance to see what might be your future. I can't even count the number of young men and women who came up here for the summer and discovered what they wanted to do with their lives. Here we are," he said, holding open the door to a large, two-storey building. As with everything else in Baddeck, it was covered in a fresh coat of white paint.

"How many live in the staff house?"

"Right now there are only nine . . . correction, you make ten. That means you get your own room. Later in the season there'll be twenty or more people, and some of you will have to double up. We haven't had as many workers since the war started, though. Mostly young boys like yourself, a few who are unfit for military service but can still swing an axe or plough a field. Rest are old codgers like me. Your room is directly at the top of the stairs. Put your things away and meet me in front of the house in fifteen minutes."

I went up the narrow stairs. Each step groaned under my weight. There was a long hall at the top and there were eight or nine closed doors. The only open door was to the room at the top of the stairs, my room. I went inside and closed the door after me. There were two beds made up with sheets, blankets and pillows. At the foot of each were two extra blankets, neatly folded. There was a writing desk, a wooden chair, a night table with a lamp on it and a chest of drawers.

I dropped my bag on the bed closer to the dresser. I looked at the bag and sadly shook my head. It was my father's old seaman's duffel bag, and I remembered how proud I'd been when he'd given it to me when he got a new one years ago. Now I saw it as nothing more than a beat-up old piece of canvas. I opened the drawstrings, pulled my clothes out and put them away in the top drawer. That was it for my unpacking. I didn't have many clothes. I was growing quickly, and my mother tried to stretch my clothes to fit me as best she could because we didn't have much money for anything new. Maybe if more of that money my father was earning aboard ship had been finding its way back to us…

I walked across the room and looked out the window. It was partially blocked by leaves and vines that ran up the side of the house, attached to a trellis. Other than that it was a good view, and I could see many of the buildings, including the main house. Even from this distance I could make out the purple flowers against the other colours in the flower bed.

My attention was caught by movement. A man on a horse, leading a second horse behind him, was coming toward the staff house. I watched for a minute until I realized it was Mr. McGregor. I hurried out of my room, down the stairs and out the front door to meet him. He trotted up and dismounted.

"Horses?" I asked.

"Best way to see things. This is a mighty big property and things are scattered all about. You take this one. His name is Limerick and he's very gentle," he said, handing me the reins.

Hesitantly I took them and climbed up onto the horse while Mr. McGregor hopped back onto the other steed. He flicked the reins and moved away. Limerick quickly fell into step beside the other horse without me needing to do anything except hold on.

"What are we going to see first?"

"I'm going to take you out to the farm. Most of what you'll eat is grown or raised right here on the property. After the farm we'll stop in at Sheepville."

"That's a strange name for a town."

Mr. McGregor chuckled. "It's not a town. That's just what we call it. Mr. Bell has spent years experimenting with sheep, trying to raise better breeders. Come on, Ginger!" he said, urging his horse to a trot.

The tour started with the farm and sheep yards and then moved on to other areas. We passed by open fields and untouched forest, crossed over streams and passed along the tops of high cliffs that dropped off to the vast salt-water lake below. Finally Mr. McGregor brought his horse to a stop and dismounted in a large apple orchard. I was as grateful for the shade and the chance to get off the horse as the horses were for the dried-up old apples they nibbled from the ground. I hadn't ever spent this much time in the saddle, and my backside felt tender.

"So what do you think of the place?" Mr. McGregor asked.

"What's to think?"

"You don't sound very impressed."

I shrugged. What was I supposed to say? "Well, it's big."

"And we've only covered a small part of it."

I hoped he wasn't planning on showing me all of it today; my backside couldn't handle that.

"There are hundreds of acres we haven't laid eyes on, still wild and treed, and many more buildings, including the laboratory. And of course we haven't seen the menagerie."

"What's a menagerie?" I asked.

"It's like a zoo."

"He has a zoo?" I was now impressed, but probably not in the way McGregor intended.

"Aye. Mr. Bell loves animals. His menagerie has different types of birds, including two bald eagles, a bobcat, a cougar and many others. 'Course it's lost my favourite animal, Bruno the bear."

"A bear?"

"A big black bear. Over seven feet tall standing on his back feet."

"What happened to him?"

"He kept breaking out of his pen."

"He escaped?" I asked.

"More than once. I still see him around the property from time to time."

"You do?"

"Oh, certainly. Haven't seen him for a while... over

two weeks . . . but he just seems to pop out when and where you least expect him. You'll see him, I'm sure."

I looked around anxiously, like I half expected the bear to materialize out of thin air.

"Maybe our next stop should be the kite house," Mr. McGregor suggested.

"There's a house for kites?"

"That's just what we call the building because in former times it was home to all of the experiments with kites that Mr. Bell was performing. There are no kites in there now. It's being used to build lifeboats under contract with the Royal Navy. Over twenty men and women work there seven days a week. You may even start there. It's important work."

"More important than playing with kites," I chuckled.

Mr. McGregor gave me a hard look. "Playing? Play had nothing to do with those kites. It was work . . . research . . . scientific experimentation."

"How is flying a kite 'scientific experimentation'?"

"Have you ever been in an airplane?"

"Of course not," I said. I was amazed the few times I'd actually seen one in the air. Lord knows how they stayed up there, but I dreamed of flying in one.

"How do you think heavier-than-air flight started? Right here at this estate is where some of the most important discoveries were made. If it weren't for those kites, we might not have airplanes today! Have you ever heard of the *Silver Dart*?" he asked.

I shook my head.

"It was right here, before my very eyes, on the ice of the lake that Mr. Bell launched the first airplane in the

British Commonwealth! And if it hadn't been for the lessons learned with those kites, it never would have been possible! Play, indeed! Now do you have any more questions, young man?" he asked in a disapproving tone.

I looked away and caught sight of a long, low structure in the distance. "Can I see that building?" I asked, pointing into the distance, hoping to change the subject.

He shook his head.

"What goes on in there?"

"Biggest thing on the estate. They're working on the hydrofoil."

"What's a hydrofoil?" I asked.

"It's a special type of boat... very special and very experimental. As experimental as the kites were. But you won't be working in there. It's all pretty hush-hush what's going on."

"I thought you were supposed to show me everything on the estate." This was the first thing about the whole place that had even remotely interested me, so of course I wasn't going to be allowed near it. I almost had to laugh; I was far from home but some things were exactly the same.

"Well..." He paused and smiled. "Maybe we can just take a peek in. You don't look like a German spy."

"A German spy?"

"I shouldn't be saying any of this. It's enough that you know that what's going on in there could be important for the war effort... I've maybe said too much. Mount up and we'll go and have a look... from a distance."

I forgot about my sore behind and quickly climbed back up onto Limerick.

The building was close to the water's edge. And as we rounded the corner I saw a sort of railroad track running out of a huge door in the side of the structure and right down into the water. We tied the horses to a tree and I followed Mr. McGregor, who paused well away from the large open door.

"This is close enough," Mr. McGregor said.

I was struck by a wave of strong, pungent fumes. "What is that smell?"

"They must be waterproofing the hull today. Awful, isn't it?" Mr. McGregor commented.

I nodded and coughed in response.

It was darker inside and it was hard for my eyes to adjust enough to see anything inside the building. I squinted and cupped a hand over the top of my eyes to block out the brightness. I could see there was a big space and in the middle was a large wooden object that looked like some sort of cross between a boat and an airplane. It was immense! It had to be more than sixty feet long, and two "wings" extended out to the sides. It sat on metal railings at the end of the railroad tracks.

"Quite a beauty, isn't she?" Mr. McGregor asked.

"Definitely different."

"Now have you seen something that has you impressed?" he asked.

Before I could answer, three men walked out of the building. They were talking so intently that they didn't notice us immediately.

"Mind your manners and I'll introduce you to some of the men in charge of this project.

"Good afternoon," Mr. McGregor called out.

They stopped talking and looked up at us.

"Gentlemen, I'd like you to meet the newest hand around the estate. He'll be working here throughout the summer. This is Billy McCracken."

They hesitated for a second, and a serious look crossed the face of the eldest of the three men.

"I'm Casey Baldwin," one of the younger men said. He came forward and shook my hand firmly.

"Casey is the principal designer... an engineer by profession," Mr. McGregor explained. "And these two fine gentlemen are William Stewart, chief carpenter at Beinn Bhreagh, and his son Murdock, whose job includes a little bit of everything with the HD-4."

Each of the men in turn shook my hand.

"Ah, and there is Mr. Bell himself!" Mr. McGregor said.

Mr. Bell came out of the big door. I was hoping not to see him face to face for at least a few days.

"Mr. Bell, this is your newest employee, Billy Mc-Cracken."

"William and I have already made an acquaintance," Mr. Bell announced very formally. "Perhaps you should be taking him around to Sheepville."

"Already done, Mr. Bell. We were just heading toward the menagerie when Billy saw this building and asked about it. I know how proud everybody is of the work going on here and—"

"Work we should be getting back to," Mr. Stewart said sharply.

"You're right, of course... I just wanted Billy to see some of the impressive things being done around the estate."

"And the HD-4 certainly is impressive, isn't she, Billy?" Casey Baldwin asked.

Mr. McGregor laughed. "Come on, Casey, he's only just seen her from a distance, and what other answer could he give with us all hovering over him?"

"Oh, don't worry about William. He'd tell you if he thought it was just some *batty* old boat," Mr. Bell said.

There was no trace of expression on his face. I'd made a lot of money reading people's faces when I was playing poker against them, but I had no idea what was going on in his head and behind the hard, strong gaze that was aimed at me. I had the awful feeling he wasn't just looking at me, but looking right through me.

"So what do you think of her?" Casey asked again, gesturing toward the boat.

"I… I don't know… I don't know anything about it," I grumbled. "I can hardly see it from here."

"Do you think you might be able to tell him a wee bit, Casey?" Mr. McGregor asked.

"Alec?" Casey asked, turning to Bell.

"A wee bit," he said, nodding his head.

Casey burst into a huge smile. "She's close to sixty feet long, powered by twin two hundred and fifty horsepower twelve-cylinder Renault engines. The maximum diameter is five-point-seven feet, tapered toward front and back, built around six wooden bulkheads with an outside skin laid spirally in marine glue—"

"That's the god-awful smell," Mr. McGregor explained.

"Her top speed should be between seventy and eighty miles per hour when she rises on her hydrofoils, which are set on a ninety-degree dihedral—"

"Casey, you're talking to a young lad, not another engineer," Mr. Bell interrupted. He turned directly to me. "Do you know what a hydrofoil is, lad?"

I shook my head.

"Have you ever skipped a rock across some water?"

"Yes," I answered blankly. Who hadn't?

"The hydrofoil is just like that rock. It skips across the surface of the water so it can move much faster than a boat travelling through the water. Do you understand?"

I nodded.

"And," Casey continued, "this will be the perfect ship to hunt down and sink—"

"I think that's more than the lad needs," Mr. Bell interrupted.

"I do get carried away," Casey said. "But I guess we should work instead of talk if we ever want to see her run."

"We won't trouble you any more, gentlemen. I've still some areas to show to Billy before we decide where he'll first be working," Mr. McGregor said.

"Why don't you start him off at Sheepville?" Mr. Bell asked.

"Sheepville?"

"As good a place as any."

"Good, then it's decided," Mr. McGregor said. "He'll start tomorrow at seven-thirty."

"I'd like you to make an exception for the first day and let him begin a little bit later," Bell said.

"Later?" Mr. McGregor questioned.

"Aye. He'll be up late tonight."

"I will?"

"I expect you up at the main house this evening to offer some assistance at the gathering."

This was going to be even worse than I thought. If it weren't bad enough that I'd be spending my days walking through sheep manure, during the evening I'd be nothing more than a servant, fetching and grovelling for a bunch of rich people who thought they were better than me. Just you wait, though, I thought, until the first chance I get when nobody's looking. I'll just go and spit in somebody's soup!

"Come, Billy, let's get moving," Mr. McGregor said.

I trailed after him but looked back over my shoulder, catching a last glimpse of that machine before we'd moved too far away to see it any more.

Chapter Five

"THERE'S NOTHING TO worry about," Mrs. McCauley-Brown said as she stood before me, straightening the shirt and tie she'd borrowed for me. She said it wouldn't be right if I wasn't dressed formally. I felt stupid and angry. I was sure this was Bell's way of humiliating me for making that comment about him. He wasn't just batty, he was downright mean-spirited.

As well as angry, I felt nervous. I could feel sweat trickling down my sides.

"All you have to do is take away the empty plates. Just remember to take from the right. You serve from the left and remove from the right. Got it?" she asked.

"Yeah, I think I can remember," I answered with a touch of sarcasm.

"Good. Now take this," she said, pressing a tray into my hands and pushing me toward the door.

I stumbled out of the kitchen and almost directly into the dining room. People were sitting around the large, rectangular table. I did a quick count; there were sixteen. Mr. Bell occupied the seat at the head of the table and his wife sat beside him. I'd met her before the first guests arrived. I'd been told to look at her when I spoke because she couldn't hear and she had to be able to read my lips. I'd never heard of people being able to do such a thing, and the way she understood everything and talked so well, I couldn't believe she was deaf.

Everybody was eating heartily, and there was a lot of lively conversation. Mr. Bell looked like he was having a good time. He roared with laughter. The only other person I recognized was Casey Baldwin. As I removed the dessert plates, Mr. Baldwin introduced me to the other visitors. Some were from Philadelphia, and some were from as far away as Washington, D.C. Other than sailors, I'd never met anyone from the United States before. And they were hanging on Mr. Bell's every word.

I helped to remove the last of the dishes, reaching over and grabbing them from the table and piling them on my tray.

Mr. Bell stood up and the conversation died as every eye turned to him.

"Ladies and gentlemen... my fine guests... with the conclusion of the meal I suggest we retire to the drawing room, where our enjoyment can be prolonged in greater comfort."

A few people echoed back agreement and his guests slowly rose to their feet. Mr. Bell walked up to my side and I swallowed hard.

"William, I'd like you to go to my bedroom. You will find a humidor… large, brown, sitting on the bookshelf by my desk. I would like you to remove a dozen cigars and bring them to the drawing room."

"I don't know where your room is."

"Through those doors near the front of the house."

I put the tray down on the table and hurried off.

"And William!" he called out.

I turned around.

"Please be gentle with the cigars. They are delicate, fine works of art."

He certainly cared for his cigars. I went down the hall and stopped in front of the closed door. Gently I pushed it open. There was a small light sitting atop a dresser and the room was bathed in a dim, yellow glow. It was a large room filled with furniture. The bed was a big four-poster covered by a thick quilt. What surprised me even more than the bedroom being on the main floor was that the room was almost completely ringed by windows. The sun had almost set but there was still enough light to clearly see the long curving driveway, and Bras d'Or Lake and the lights of Baddeck in the distance.

I couldn't help but think that his bedroom had the same view of the water as mine. Of course that was the only thing the two rooms shared—the only thing that the two of us did, or ever would, have in common.

This bedroom was bigger than the entire flat where my whole family lived. It just didn't seem fair that one man could have so much… just not fair.

I turned my attention away from the windows and back to the room. A large writing desk sat in the corner.

Behind it, occupying an entire wall, was an enormous bookcase. The lone shelf not devoted to books housed what I hoped was the humidor.

I removed the lid and the smell of tobacco filled my nose. Inside were dozens and dozens of cigars. Carefully I removed one and examined it. It was long and thick and brown and had a paper wrapper around the end. I read the wrapper: Cuba. I'd only smoked a few times and I really didn't know much about cigars and smoking, although Tim and most of my new friends smoked. There was always a haze of smoke hovering over top of any poker game I'd seen or played in. But I did know that the most expensive cigars in the world came from Cuba.

I counted out and removed another eleven cigars until I had an even dozen. I was going to put the lid back on the humidor when I was struck by a thought: there were so many cigars in there that he wouldn't know if a few were missing, and I might be able to sell them. Maybe I'd even try to smoke one. I hadn't enjoyed the few cigarettes I'd smoked, but it might be different with a cigar. I reached back in and drew out two, hesitated and took a third. I put the lid back on the humidor. I tried to put them into one of my pockets, but they were too long. I removed them and gingerly tucked them into the front of my pants. They'd be fine there until I got to my room.

I walked out of the room and closed the door behind me. I felt the cigars digging into my leg and shortened my stride so I wouldn't break them. I opened the door to the drawing room and was surprised to see the furniture had been cleared away to the sides of the room and in its place four folding tables had appeared. The guests started to take seats at the chairs, four to each table. Then, to my utter amazement, decks of cards were brought to the tables. They were going to play cards!

"I'll take one of those," Casey said, putting a hand on my shoulder.

"What?" I asked, dumfounded, staring around the room.

"The cigars. I'll take one."

"Oh, yeah," I answered, handing him a cigar. "You're all going to play cards?" I asked, although it seemed pretty obvious what was going on.

"Yes, bridge. Have you ever played?"

"It's a very ingenious game," Mr. Bell added, coming up from behind me.

"I... no... I've never heard of it."

"There is a great deal of strategy involved, not unlike playing poker, but with a partner. Are you familiar with poker?" Mr. Bell questioned.

"Oh sure, I know..." I stopped. "I know a little bit about poker... I saw some men playing it once."

I had almost blabbed out what a good player I was. It was always wrong to brag about being good at anything, but doubly wrong when it was poker. It worked to your advantage to let people think you didn't know the game; after all, how could somebody who didn't know how to play cheat or hustle? It was better if they just thought you had "beginner's luck." It was safer for the guy you took to be mad at Lady Luck than at you.

"I want you to pass out the cigars to the gentlemen and then come and pull up a seat right beside me. I'll explain the game to you as we play. Learning to play bridge should be part of every young man's education," Mr. Bell said.

"You want me to sit beside you?"

"Yes, when you're finished I expect you to pull up a chair."

I slowly handed out the cigars. What was he up to, and what did he want from me? He probably just wanted to impress me with how smart he was, I guessed. Or maybe I was there to fetch and carry for him.

I pulled a chair over and sat down just off to the side. As I did, I could feel the stolen cigars breaking, but there wasn't much I could do. The cards were shuffled and dealt until they were all distributed. That meant each player had been given thirteen cards. I was close enough to see Bell's cards cradled in his hands. I noticed immediately that nobody seemed to be shielding their cards very well; if I leaned ever so slightly over to one side I was sure I'd be able to see the cards of the person sitting beside me.

"Now, William, in bridge each person has a partner who sits opposite to his seat. So in this game my partner is my lovely wife."

Mrs. Bell smiled softly and nodded her head. "You'll have to be patient with my husband, William. He may be an inventor by profession but he is first and foremost a teacher."

"And the lesson has begun. In bridge, working with your partner you must attempt to take "tricks," that's a round of cards played, in order to obtain points toward winning the hand. The secret is not only to be aware of the cards you hold but to know what cards are in your partner's hand."

Sounded an awful lot like poker, except for the partner part. "Can you let your partner know your hand through signals?" I asked.

"No, no, my dear boy!" the woman sitting beside me exclaimed. "That wouldn't be fair now would it?"

"Don't be so hard on the lad," Bell cautioned. "He is in fact correct."

"He is?" the woman said.

"Of course. By the manner in which my partner plays her cards, as well as the way she responds to bidding, I can be reasonably certain which cards she is holding. William, I want you to watch this game closely."

They began playing. They exchanged comments about "trumps" and "no trumps" which made no sense to me, and then the person to the left of the dealer started playing her cards.

The first few hands passed without me making any sense of or seeing any order to their actions. Occasionally Mr. Bell would lean back and mutter a few words to me, which just added to the mystery. My mind strained to try to assign order to the game. Little glimmers of understanding would start to form, and then just as quickly the next move would show them to be wrong. I tried to see the pattern to the bidding and an order in the way the cards were played. I made guesses, some of which were right, about which cards were held by Bell's partner. The game ended with Mr. and Mrs. Bell winning. They remained seated at the table and their original opponents left and were replaced by another pair. All around the room people were rotating from table to table to play against other partners. I watched intently through three complete games.

"I think it's time for William to be turning in for the night," Mrs. Bell said.

"Turning in? It's hardly ten-thirty!" Bell protested. "He has much to learn here tonight!"

"He'll learn more tomorrow after a good night's sleep. It's been a long day."

Bell scowled at his wife's words and then his whole face softened. "Aye, you're right, and it has been a long day. The lessons in bridge can continue another time. Everyone should bid a goodnight to young William," he announced.

I rose to my feet and mumbled good nights in response to their waves and comments.

There had been a friendliness to their voices—in fact, everybody had been very nice to me all night long, not like the way I expected rich people to treat the servants. I almost felt a little bad about taking the cigars—almost.

I pushed through the door into the kitchen. Mrs. McCauley-Brown was at the sink washing the last of what must have been a mountain of dishes.

"So, you see, there was nothing to be nervous about," she said.

"I wasn't nervous."

"Whatever you say," she said in a tone that made me think she didn't believe me. "Now come and sit down. I'm going to fix us both a cup of tea. I still haven't had time to read this correspondence from your mother," she said, pulling the letter out of the pocket of her apron.

"Probably nothing more than a mother bragging about her son, is all it is."

I hoped that was all it was. I really didn't have any idea what my mother had told or written her friend. I knew she'd been concerned by some of the things I'd done, and afraid of others she believed I was doing, but I sure hoped she was too embarrassed to share them.

She started opening the letter. "What's this?" she asked as she pulled out both a letter and another envelope. She held the envelope in her hand and examined it. "This is for you," she said, handing it to me.

It had my name written on the front in my mother's flowing writing. Why would she be sending me a letter?

"Probably just wants to tell you how much she already misses you," Mrs. McCauley-Brown said, answering my unspoken question.

Of course she must be right. I tucked the letter into my pocket so I could read it later.

"Just as I suspected. Hardly gets through the first three lines of the letter before she's telling me what a whiz you are in school!"

I guess she didn't write about how I was almost tossed out of school this past year for not going to classes. There were better things to do and better ways to learn how to make money. I'd never had one single teacher explain how to palm a pair of dice or how to deal off the bottom of the deck. All the teachers I'd ever had knew lots about book learning but nothing about the world outside their classrooms. Besides, if playing cards was good enough for my father, why wasn't it good enough for me?

She continued to read until the whistling kettle roused her to her feet. She poured a bit of the steaming water into a teapot and swirled it around before dumping it down the sink. Next she popped a tea ball into the pot and filled it with the remaining water. She set it down in front of me and brought over two cups and saucers, a sugar bowl and a small pitcher of milk.

"Let it steep while I finish up the letter."

She read quickly, running her finger down the page, occasionally nodding her head or chuckling to herself. She put the letter down and looked up at me.

"It's good your mother is doing well. I can only imagine how hard it has been for her, and for you, since the start of the war. It must be terrible to have your father gone so much, and you all must worry so much." She paused. "Your mother told me about the problems you've been having. It'll be good for you to be here for the summer, and away from… influences."

I looked down at my hands. I guess she knew more than I'd wanted her to know.

She put her hands on top of mine. "It'll all work out. You'll see. Why don't you just finish up your tea while I check to make sure things are all put away in the dining room."

I took a sip and then remembered my letter. I pulled it out and ripped off the end. It seemed to me I was a bit too old to miss my mother, but I was still looking forward to hearing from her, and I hoped that the letter would bring a little comfort.

Dear William,

I know you're still probably angry with me about the arrangement for you to spend the summer in Baddeck. I am sorry but there is no choice. I felt, and still feel, that to be here for the summer would only result in you being led further down the wrong road. I know that in the back of your head you simply thought you'd try it out for a week or so and if it didn't work you'd return. But you cannot return home. You must make it work. You must listen to directions, mind your tongue and work hard.

If you are dismissed and asked to leave, then you may not return to my home or to Halifax. If you were to show up at my door before the end of August I would turn you away. I would then contact the police and make arrangements for you to be arrested as a vagrant. It would break my heart, and perhaps I would lose you, but I cannot risk your loss without a fight.

William, you are my son and I love you more than life itself. I cannot sit back and see you throw away your life. I know it's hard for all for us. Please, let's not make it any more difficult.

With much love,
Mother

The shock I'd felt earlier in the day when I realized it was Bell I was talking to was nothing compared to what I now felt. I let the letter fall to the floor. What was she saying? How could she not let me come home? I could understand my father turning me away, but my mother? This made no sense. I stood up, grabbed the letter from the floor and rushed out of the room before Mrs. McCauley-Brown could return.

I moved quickly along the path leading to the staff house. The moon was full and bright, but was almost completely blocked by the clouds that filled the sky. I hated the dark, but for once I was grateful because it let me hide so no one could see me.

"Darn!" I said out loud as I felt one of the cigars crunch against my leg. I reached a hand down my pants to retrieve them. One was broken completely in two, while a second was badly bent and the third was more or less intact. I knew I wouldn't be able to get to sleep right away, what with my mind being filled with the letter and all the things that had happened today. Maybe I should go and see what all the fuss was about with these cigars.

I looked around. This was definitely not the spot to smoke one of them. I remembered the vine-covered arbour that was across the field from the staff house. It offered protection as well as a place to sit. I left the path and crossed over the lawn. My feet quickly became wet from the dew clinging to the grass. The clouds parted and the whole landscape became illuminated, leaving me feeling exposed to any eyes that might be watching. I hurried my pace, feeling safe only once I had stepped into the shadows. I moved along the path. There were trees and bushes on both sides and the branches over-hanging the top gave it the feel of a tunnel. The moon was visible through the branches but then suddenly dis-appeared once again behind the clouds, and the dark became darker. I went farther into the safety of the arbour until I reached a large, solid, wooden bench where I took a seat. My bottom was still a little sore from the horse, but it did feel good to be sitting.

I put the cigar in my mouth and dug into my pocket to remove a box of matches I'd lifted from the kitchen. I struck the match on the side of the box and it came to life, casting a light I hoped wouldn't escape the vines. I held it up to the end of the stogie and sucked in strongly to ignite it. Nothing. I sucked harder and harder but couldn't get it to light. The match burned down close to my fingers and I blew it out and threw it to the ground. I pulled out another match and tried again. I could feel the sulphurous fumes of the match being drawn through the cigar and into my lungs, but it wouldn't catch. I'd been sucking so hard I almost felt a little light-headed.

I removed the cigar from my mouth. Why wasn't it lighting? Then I remembered how I'd seen the men tonight use a little clipper to take off the end of the cigars before they lit them. Somehow this step must be needed before it could be lit. Maybe if I bit the end off, which was now soggy, it would…

I heard a sound and turned toward the noise. Quickly I moved to hide the evidence of my crime. I stuffed the matches back into my pocket and threw the cigar into the bushes. It wasn't the noise of feet against the gravel path but the sound of somebody moving through the bushes. Why would somebody be walking through the bushes… or was it something? My mind was filled with the image of Bruno the bear, his massive black body pushing aside the brush, his nose to the ground searching

for food. After being in the kitchen all evening, I was
sure I smelled of whatever he was looking for.

As quietly as I could, I slipped off the bench and slid
underneath it, pulling my legs out of sight. I held my
breath and strained my eyes, listening for the approach-
ing animal. There was nothing. Maybe I hadn't heard
anything, or maybe it had just been the sound of wind
rustling through the leaves, or a rabbit foraging for food. I
was glad nobody was there to see me hiding under a
bench, afraid of a rabbit. What did I know about animals?
I grew up in Halifax and had never left the city more
than a few miles behind my whole life.

I reached my hands up to pull myself out from under
the bench when the quiet was broken by the sound of a
whistle. I turned my head toward the sound. A few seconds later a second whistle, a different tone and coming
from the other direction, answered back. There was
another pause of a half dozen seconds and then the first
whistle repeated itself. What was going on? The night air
was now rumbling with the sound of feet moving along
the gravel walkway, toward where I lay under the bench.
I couldn't be sure but it seemed to be coming from both
directions. The sound of the crunching gravel became
louder and louder, and then my eyes grew wide as I saw
a pair of feet, and then a second set, stop directly in front
of the bench. I drew myself back as far away from the
path as I could.

I heard two male voices, and although they were talking quietly, it was just loud enough for me to hear.
Instinctively I closed my eyes to try and make out the
words. Both men turned and sat on the bench. It creaked

noisily under the strain of their weight and for a split second I had a terrible image of it crashing down on top of me. They continued to talk, and I realized that while I could hear the words I didn't understand what they meant. They weren't speaking English. What language were they speaking?

I looked up and through one of the small gaps in the boards of the bench I could make out the shadowy outline of one of the men. I could see he was wearing some sort of hat. I turned my attention to the only part of them I could really see, their feet. One man wore a pair of old and worn canvas work shoes. The second had on a pair of high boots. They reminded me of the ones Mr. McGregor had worn that morning when we were riding the horses, except these were shiny and expensive looking.

The voices became louder, and while I couldn't understand the words I knew that they were disagreeing about something.

"Please, please be quiet!" one of the men pleaded in English. "We must not be discovered!"

The other voice became silent and then started speaking much more softly in the foreign language. They continued their discussion, but in a much more gentle tone.

My mind raced, trying to figure out who these men were and what were they doing out here. Suddenly the back of one of the boots slid back and touched against my chest. I stifled the natural instinct to cry out. He didn't know I was there, he was simply shifting his feet.

Ever so slowly and silently I repositioned myself to move away from the boots. I inched sideways until my entire body was crunched down into just one half of the bench. I looked back up and could see a gap between where the two men sat, still talking. I saw a flash of white go from one man to the other.

They rose to their feet. They were standing only a foot or two apart.

"Do not fail," a voice called out. Although it was English the words were said with a heavy accent.

"I will do my job."

"We are counting on you to keep that promise. Promises must be kept."

The boots turned and started away down the path, while the other feet stood still watching. The crunching of the gravel faded into nothing; it was completely silent, and I held my breath. Finally, after what seemed like a long time but was probably only half a minute, the second figure turned and walked away in the other direction. I listened for the sound of those feet to fade away as well.

Satisfied that I was alone, I continued to lie under the bench. I had no way of knowing how far they'd gone. All I did know was that something was going on here. Something a lot more serious than me stealing three cigars.

Chapter Six

"WHAT'S GOING ON?" Isaac yelled.

The group of men, some standing and the rest on their knees, parted slightly to allow Isaac, the foreman at Sheepville, through.

"Dice? You're playing dice?" he asked incredulously.

I scooped the dice off the floor, leaving the coins and a couple of bills sitting in front of the players.

"And worst yet, gambling!"

People seemed to edge slightly away, as though they were trying to distance themselves from the action.

"This isn't what you're paid to do. All of you get back to work!"

"Come on, Isaac, it's our lunch break," one of the men, Samuel, protested.

"Lunch break or not, you have to stop playing."

The Hydrofoil Mystery 65

"I'm down too much money to stop now," Samuel said.

"Me too!" added a second.

"And me as well!" a third voice complained.

"You can't all be losing. Somebody has to be winning."

"Somebody is… the kid."

Isaac looked at me with that look of disapproval I'd come to know so well during my week and a half working at Sheepville. He was always on me, accusing me of "slacking off," or not being "careful" or not taking enough "pride in my work." What sort of idiot could take pride in shovelling sheep manure, or piling hay, or throwing feed to a bunch of mindless, bleating sheep?

"And how much is he up?" Isaac asked.

"Not that much… a dollar or two."

Although I was careful not to count my winnings I knew it was close to nine dollars. I cupped my dice in my hands.

"Pretty lucky, aren't you, boy?"

"I guess so," I answered.

Actually luck had nothing to do with my winning. These dice were "loaded." They were specially weighted so one would roll a three and the other a four for an unbeatable seven. When it was my turn to throw the dice, I used my "lucky" pair, and then when it was somebody else's turn I "palmed" this pair and exchanged them with an identical set. Well, identical in appearance but not in action; the second set was a real pair, which land equally on all sides.

The secret was to exchange them smoothly and effortlessly so nobody even suspected I was changing dice. I'd once heard of a guy in Halifax who was winning big time when the rest of the gamblers started getting suspicious. They could never see him make the exchange but he kept winning. Finally four or five of them grabbed him and started searching through his clothes. They didn't find the second set of dice until they'd pretty well stripped him down to his underwear. I heard how he then got a "swimming lesson" off a pier, into the harbour, at night, in November. That thought made me shiver like I was feeling the freezing water myself.

"And whose dice are they, anyway?" Isaac asked.

I didn't like the tone of his voice or where this might be leading.

"Maybe I'm just an old fool, but my father always told me to never trust a winner when it's his deck of cards or dice."

I swallowed hard.

"Come on, Isaac. Make sense," Sam said. "Are you accusing the kid of cheating us?"

"I'm not saying anything," he said, although obviously he was.

"Yeah, Isaac, you think we haven't been watching?" one of the others continued. "Besides, dice are dice."

"Haven't you lads ever heard of fixed dice?"

"Fixed?"

"Yes. Dice all done up to land on certain numbers."

"Like seven?" Samuel asked.

"Of course like seven. Nobody wants their dice to land on snake-eyes."

Samuel looked at me hard. "So with special dice like

that somebody could throw a seven three times in a row, is that right?"

I felt sweat start running down my sides. I'd just thrown three sevens in a row.

" 'Course he could! Three, four or even five hundred times in a row," Isaac answered with a cackle.

"But how come when we use the dice we don't roll sevens?" asked another man.

Half the eyes looked up at Isaac while the rest continued to stare at me. I couldn't risk exchanging the dice.

"Now, I'm not saying the boy is doing this," Isaac began, although again it was clear he was saying exactly that, "but I've heard tell of people switching dice. They have two pairs on them, one for themselves to throw and a second set for the rest of the players."

Now every eye was on me. I looked up at Isaac. He was enjoying seeing me twist in the wind like this. I was as good as dead.

"What a joke! What a good joke!" boomed a voice.

I turned around and saw Simon peering between two of the men. I was surprised to see him there because he didn't work in Sheepville. He was a gardener and lived in the staff house two doors down from my room. He was one of the few people who were friendly to me.

"Isaac, you old coot, you really had them all going. Imagine, convincing all these men they'd been cheated by this lad… imagine," he laughed.

"How else can you explain him winning our money and throwing three sevens in a row?"

"Maybe he's lucky," Simon answered.

"Three times in a row sounds like more than luck," Isaac said.

"Are you accusing the boy of cheating?" Simon challenged.

"I didn't say that," Isaac replied.

"Luck or cheating. I see no other options," Simon countered. "And I think it is just luck… and I'm willing to bet on it." Simon, who was bigger than most of the other men, shouldered his way through the crowd and stopped right beside me.

"I am willing to make a small wager," Simon said.

"A wager?"

"A bet. I am willing to bet Billy *will not* throw a seven. Are you willing to bet that he will, Isaac?"

"Well… I… don't know if…"

"If Isaac doesn't want to bet, how about the rest of you? If you're so certain he's cheating and using loaded dice, then put your money where your mouth is. Anybody interested?"

There was a mumbling of conversation but nobody spoke up to take Simon's offer.

"Okay, everybody, break is over," Isaac spoke up. "Everybody get back to work!"

The mumbling was replaced by grumbling and complaining. The men who were just spectators started to move away. The five on their knees, who were down money, didn't budge, though.

"Go," Simon said.

Relieved, I tried to rise to my feet but was stopped by Simon's hand on my shoulder.

"I mean, go… roll the dice."

"But…but…"

"I know there's no bet, but just do it anyway to prove to them you weren't cheating."

"Yeah, go ahead," Isaac said. A few of the people who'd started to walk away turned around to watch.

I looked at Simon and then at Isaac. I pulled back my left hand and let the dice fly. At that same instant, while every pair of eyes followed the dice, I took my right hand and tucked it into the side of my pants, dumping the "lucky" pair into my underpants.

"Nine!" Simon yelled out.

He offered me a hand and pulled me to my feet. The remaining crowd quickly dispersed, but not without a fair amount of quiet cursing and grumbling.

"I guess I better get back to work too," I offered.

"Wait!" Isaac called out.

He walked toward me. He was old and wasn't very big, hardly as tall as my eyes, but he was a stubborn and cantankerous old bird and I was unnerved by him.

"Don't you want your dice?" he asked, holding out his hand.

"Thanks," I said, reaching out to take them.

He dropped the dice into my open palm and then grasped my wrist tightly. He stared into my eyes. "Peculiar how you reached out with your right hand to take the dice, but threw them with your left hand… very peculiar indeed."

I pulled my hand away but couldn't escape his gaze.

"Knowing something and proving it are two different

things. I *know* what was happening here, and I expect this will be the last I see of these dice," he said and turned and walked away.

I watched and waited until he was out of earshot. "What's his problem anyway? He's given me nothing but grief since I first got here."

"That is not surprising," Simon replied. "He does not like strangers very much, especially those from the city."

"The city? What's he got against Halifax?"

"Nothing against the city itself... just against people who come from that city... or at least one person," Simon answered.

"What do you mean?"

"It is a long story. Come, I'll explain it all as we walk to the orchard."

"The orchard?"

"Yes, that is why I'm here. I was told to come and get you on my way to the orchard."

"You mean I get to leave here!" I exclaimed.

"That is what I was told. Will you be sad?" he chuckled.

"No way! I've had enough of sheep manure to last me a lifetime."

"Good. It is perhaps good timing for you to leave. Most of the men know you did not cheat them, but it is hard to predict what people will do."

Simon turned and started off and I fell into stride beside him.

"Do you know what we're going to be doing?"

"I know I will be tending to some new trees and cutting back some of the older growth. I do not know what you will be doing."

"I didn't know you did trees. I just thought you tended to the flowers and things," I said.

"Flowers, vegetables, trees. Anything that is growing. I learned all about these things from my father, who learned from his father."

I couldn't help but think about the things I'd learned from my father—and what little good they'd ever do me.

"Your family isn't from around here, is it?" I said, commenting on his accent, which was different from the Scottish burr of a lot of the workers at the estate.

"No. My father is Dutch. Most of the gardeners are from Holland, although Mr. Bell has staff who are from many different countries. Some employers only want people to work for them who are from their own country. Mr. Bell does not care about such things. He only sees the man, not where the man is from. Which leads us back to the story I promised you about Isaac. Do you want to hear it?"

"Definitely."

"Her name was Henrietta."

"Whose name was Henrietta?"

"The woman who Isaac loved. She was from Marble Mountain, a community not far from here."

"Yeah?"

"Well, Isaac was courting Henrietta, hoping to someday make her his wife. I was told she was a very handsome woman."

"Then why would she be interested in Isaac?" I asked.

"He was not always old and wrinkled, you know. This was all much before my time here, but I am sure at one point in time he was a fine-looking young man, and she did return his interest."

"So they got married?"

"They were to marry, but alas, it was not to be. While making arrangements for the wedding she met a man... a man from the city... and he swept her off her feet. She ran off with him in the middle of the night."

"Good for her, getting away from both Isaac and that hick town!"

"Poor Isaac could not believe she had left either him or Marble Mountain. He said she would come to her senses and return and he would wait for her."

"And?"

"He's still waiting," Simon chuckled.

"I guess that explains Isaac, but what about some of the others?"

"Come now, I am sure not everybody has treated you badly."

"Not everybody. Casey and Mrs. McCauley-Brown and Mr. McGregor and a couple of the other staff in the house and you..."

"And Mr. Bell, surely?"

"I don't know if you could call it friendly. He's pretty unusual."

"Yes, he is. Geniuses almost always are, and he is a true genius. You have to remember, this is a very small community. I've been here more than fifteen years and am still seen as an outsider, so you can hardly expect to fit in after a few days."

"I don't want to fit in!" I protested.

"Which may explain part of the problem. I know this

is not your home, and from your attitude and comments I understand you do not wish to be here, but you must remember, when you say negative things or comments about being here you are also insulting the people who live here… in these, how did you say, hick towns."

"I wasn't trying to insult anybody."

"Maybe not trying… but you have succeeded anyway. People are proud of where they are from. They cannot easily separate themselves from the place where they were born. When you say disparaging things about Baddeck, you cannot help but belittle them. Try to keep a little distance between yourself and Isaac for the next few days. Okay?"

"Believe me, if I had my way I'd keep some distance from him for the next few decades."

I decided to follow Simon's advice and stayed away from the staff house that night by helping out Mrs. McCauley-Brown in the kitchen and then staying there to eat a late supper. It was almost ten o'clock and most of the men, some of whom got up as early as five in the morning to start work, would be fast asleep. I said my goodnights and headed across the field to turn in. I figured I'd get up the stairs so quickly that even if the noise did wake somebody up I'd be in my room before they got up to investigate.

The black of the sky was punctured by a million shining stars, and the brilliant full moon lit a path for me. It was almost as bright as a road in Halifax, lit up with gas street lamps.

The windows of the staff house were all darkened and

there was no sound except for the chirping of the crickets. It looked like my plan had worked. Quietly I opened the door and bumped into something. I looked up and found myself staring up into the eyes of a bear!

"AAAAAAHHHH!" I screamed and stumbled, landing heavily on the ground. I scrambled backwards, expecting the bear to come charging toward me, but instead it just stood there on its back legs, threatening with its claws, not moving, like . . . I heard laughter coming from the windows above my head.

"Goodnight, Billy, and don't forget to take the bear for a walk," a voice floated out of the darkness, accompanied by more laughter.

On trembling legs I pulled myself to my feet. The bear stood there in the doorway, as still as a statue—or as still as a stuffed bear. Cautiously I moved toward the beast.

"What're you worried about... it won't be biting you!" somebody else yelled down, followed by more laughter.

I pushed past the stuffed black bear, which towered over my head. I ran up the stairs, into my room and slammed the door behind me. I wanted to just throw myself into bed, but first I had to change. I'd wet myself.

Chapter Seven

July 8, 1917

Dear Mother,

*I hope everything is going well for you and Sarah.
I am doing all right. This first week has been like a
blur. I've been working all around the estate. Sometimes I help in the house, other times out on the farm,
or chopping wood, or running errands. I'm not too
sure how any of this is supposed to build my "char-
acter," but I can tell you that this place certainly is
filled with characters. Maybe the strangest of them all
is Mr. Bell himself; he's downright different and the
locals think he's "batty."*

*The only interesting thing going on here involves
them working on a special type of boat called a hydrofoil. It looks like a gigantic cigar with wings more
than it does a boat. It is powered by not one, but two,
aircraft engines. I heard that when they turn on the*

engines the sound inside the building is enough to rattle the fillings right out of your teeth. But it doesn't really matter though, because it's the one place on the whole estate where they won't let me work. I'm good enough to shovel sheep manure or weed gardens, or cut wood or even work as a helper when they're throwing fancy parties for their fancy friends, but not good enough to work on the hydrofoil. I really don't care anyway. I hear that the people working on it never take any breaks and work a lot longer than the rest of us. Because today is Saturday I only have to work until two o'clock in the afternoon, and those people working on the hydrofoil will keep on working while I'm in town having fun (don't worry, I'll have safe fun). I just thought I should write before going. I'll write again next week.

Billy

P.S. I have a room to myself, the food is good and Mrs. McCauley-Brown sends her regards.

I put the pen down on the desk and closed the lid on the ink. Deliberately I hadn't said anything about my father. It was doubtful he was at home and even if he was I didn't have anything I wanted to say to him. I fanned the letter in the air to dry the ink before I folded it and sealed it in an envelope. After the letter she'd written to me I didn't really want to write her, but I had no choice. Mrs. McCauley-Brown had told me she wasn't going to give me my pay packet until I showed her a letter to my mother. I waved it in the air a few times, figuring that should dry it enough. A few little bits of smudging wouldn't stop my mother from being able to read it or me from getting paid.

I'd heard from a couple of the other workers who lived in Baddeck that I could expect some cards or dice to be going on in one of the back rooms of the hotel. I looked at myself in the mirror. The way I looked was important. I had to look old enough to get into the game, but young enough that the other players would see me as a "mark." It wasn't going to be like on the train. I'd been so anxious to win that I'd forgotten half of what I'd learned. Tonight I'd be patient and wait for the right time. Being greedy or in a hurry only leads to trouble.

I opened the top drawer of my dresser, moved aside underwear and pulled out my dice. I hadn't used them around the estate since that last game up at Sheepville, but that didn't mean I couldn't use them in town. I squeezed them for luck and then secured them safely in my pocket. Next I stuffed the letter in the envelope and hurried down the stairs and toward the main house. Hopefully not just my pay, but also a ride to town would be waiting there—I didn't want to waste another minute.

"Hold still!" Mrs. McCauley-Brown ordered as she took a facecloth and scrubbed away at some dirt she'd spied on my cheek.

"Come on, you're taking off skin!" I protested, but she continued to scour away.

"Just a little bit more. There, clean enough to go to town." She crossed the kitchen and dropped the cloth in the sink. "I imagine this is what you've been waiting for," she said, pulling out a brown envelope, my pay packet, from her pocket.

"Thank you," I said, taking it from her. I ripped the

top off and dumped the contents in my hands. I counted out eleven dollars. It was far from a fortune but it was a handsome amount and it would give me the bankroll I needed.

"Before you go, I need to talk to you, Billy."

"Sure."

"Sit down, please."

I hesitated; my time in town was ticking away.

"Don't worry, you'll still have time in Baddeck," she said, reading my mind.

Reluctantly I sat down and she pulled up a chair beside me.

"You know your mother and I go back a long time. Oh, the stories I could tell you about the good old days we shared..." She paused. "But that's not what I need to talk to you about."

Thank goodness, I thought.

"You were given this job on my recommendation. Dozens and dozens of young men apply to work here each summer. It's quite an honour to be selected."

I didn't see how coming up here and mucking stables and chopping wood could be seen as any sort of honour, even if the pay was good.

"And your performance is a reflection upon me and my recommendation. And thus far I have received complaints."

"Complaints? About what?"

"Your attitude, your work habits, your laziness."

"I know who complained. That old man at the farm wanted me to do all the work while he just sat there on the wagon!"

"If you mean Isaac, yes, he has voiced concern. As has almost everybody with whom you've come in contact. Complaints have been registered across the estate."

"Everybody's complained? They're just mad at me because…" I stopped. I didn't think it was smart to tell her they were angry with me because I took some of their money playing dice.

"Some of them are mad at you over the gambling, but that isn't why they complained. And not everybody has complained, but only two people have had good things to say about your work."

One had to be Simon, but who was the second?

"I want you to be on your best behaviour in town today."

I didn't answer. She reached forward and placed a hand on my shoulder. "It hasn't been easy for you, Billy. I know things have changed since the war, with your father gone most of the time and—"

"You don't know nothing!" I yelled, jumping to my feet.

"Billy!"

I was filled with a rush of anger and pushed out the door and ran down across the porch and off down the laneway. I ran quickly, not looking back. I didn't need a ride to town, and I certainly didn't need to hear anything she had to say. All I needed was right in my pocket: my bankroll and a pair of dice. I didn't stop running until I'd cleared the front gate and set foot on the road to town.

I slowed to a walk, panting to get my breath. Why did I care what any of these people thought, anyway? What did I care what anybody thought? So they didn't think I was

doing a good job, so what? The worst they could do was
fire me! Even if I couldn't go back to Halifax right away, I
could find someplace else to go. Part of me wanted to
leave right now. What was there here for me, anyway?
Wouldn't it be better to quit instead of waiting around to
be fired? I didn't even need to go back for the few things
that were in my room. They were practically worthless
anyway—worthless, like everything I'd ever had.

I heard the sound of an automobile coming up the
road behind me. I held out my thumb, hoping to hitch a
ride. The car slowed down and before it came to a stop I
recognized the driver; it was Casey Baldwin, the engineer working on the hydrofoil. Other than meeting him
on that first day at the boathouse, and then at the party
that night, I'd seen him only in passing. He always
seemed to be working.

The car pulled over to the side of the road up ahead
and I ran to it.

"Need a ride, kid?" he asked as I climbed in.

"Thanks."

The car started back into motion. It was a nice car, new
and shiny. I noticed that Casey wasn't dressed for going
to town—he was still wearing his old work clothing.

"Are you going to Baddeck?" I asked.

"I have to pick up some new equipment that came in
on the *Blue Hill* today… things I need. I'm anxious to get
it and get back to the boathouse."

"You're going to keep working on it today?"

"Today, tonight and tomorrow. But, to be truthful, I
don't think of it as work."

"You don't?"

"No," he said, shaking his head. "It's never work to do things you love doing. I wanted to join up, fight over in Europe, when war was declared. But Alec convinced me that my efforts would be better spent here, working on the HD-4. It's the most important thing I could be doing right now. Sure, it seems like I never get a break, but on the other hand, I don't think I've worked a single day since I came up to Beinn Bhreagh."

"I can't say the same thing. It all seems like work to me... and according to the talk I hear, I'm not doing it very well." Why was I saying any of this to him?

"Funny, Alec seems to think you're doing a fine job."

"Alec?"

"Mr. Bell."

"Mr. Bell said I was doing good?" I asked in disbelief.

"Yes. He was very complimentary about your work at the party and was impressed by how quickly you picked up the game of bridge."

"I can't believe he had anything good to say about me."

"Just because you called him batty?" Casey asked and started to laugh.

I felt so embarrassed. I didn't think Bell would have repeated my comment to anybody.

"Alec chuckled about that for days. Don't be fooled. He's one difficult book to read by the cover. I've known the man for a long while and most of the time I can't figure out what's going on inside that head of his."

"How long have you been here?"

"A long time. After university I came up to spend a summer, just like you, and never left. Funny how things turn out differently than we might expect. Well, here we are. Where do you want to be dropped off?"

"I don't know. Where would be a good place?" I asked.

"Main Street is where most of the activity happens."

"It's hard to believe Baddeck even has a main street," I laughed.

"Oh, it's not London or Paris or even Toronto—"

"It's not even Halifax," I interrupted.

"Or even Halifax, but there are things to keep a young man amused."

"Things like what?"

"Well, if I were a lad of fifteen or so I think I'd browse the shops, maybe buy something small to send to my mother when I mailed her a letter... the post office is just beside the courthouse, by the way. Maybe I'd catch an early evening show at the cinema, have a bite at the restaurant and top it all off with an ice cream soda. Who knows, I might even meet some of the local people... perhaps even a pretty young girl my age," he said, turning to face me with a big smile on his face.

He pulled the car over and came to a stop directly in front of the courthouse.

"Have fun, but be careful. Most of the people are friendly, but a few of the old-time locals still don't take too kindly to us outsiders."

"Outsiders?" I asked.

"Anybody who wasn't born and raised in Baddeck or the county. Even after all these years, some of the people still see Alec and his wife that way, so you mustn't be surprised if they view the likes of you and me with a suspicious eye."

That was exactly what Simon had said. "I'll be care-ful," I said to humour him, although having grown up around the docks and warehouses of Halifax I didn't think there was anything here I had to fear.

I climbed out of the car and leaned back in through the open window. "Thanks for the ride. You're going to be working on the hydrofoil tomorrow, right?"

"Tomorrow and every day until it's finished."

"Do you think you could use a hand?" I asked.

"You've been working hard all week, you should take advantage of your Sunday off."

"That's okay, I'd like to help." I could see the brush-off coming a mile away.

"I appreciate your offer, but I'm afraid that isn't possi-ble, Billy. It's all pretty technical work."

"Maybe I could clean up or get things…"

"I'm sorry, Billy, it's just that it's all so hush-hush. I know it sounds silly, but we can't have just anybody—"

"It's no big deal," I interrupted.

"I'd like nothing better than to have you come and help out. I know it sounds like something out of a dime-store novel, but—"

"Don't worry. I'd rather sleep in."

"Now you're just rubbing it in," he laughed. "I'll be up there and working by seven in the morning while you'll be sleeping. Hardly fair, is it?"

He was right about that, but what in life was fair?

"Take care, and have a good day," Casey said.

He pulled away from the sidewalk and started off down the road. Maybe he was friendlier than Bell, but it all meant the same. They thought so little of me that they didn't even want me around when I was offering to work for nothing.

Forget them! Forget that fancy boat of theirs! I was in town to have a good time!

Baddeck was much busier than when I'd first arrived. Along with Casey's automobile were half a dozen others, either parked or driving, as well as a multitude of wagons and horses. The sidewalk was crowded and people had to push past along the narrow planks.

"Billy!" a voice called out.

I turned and saw Herbie crossing the street, waving a hand at me. I couldn't say I wasn't happy to see him coming.

"I told you we'd run into each other. Do you have the time to buy an old man a cup of coffee?"

"Nope, not a cup of coffee," I answered. "But maybe a piece of pie and a cup of coffee. Where's the best place in town to eat?"

"I can show you the best place, but I'm afraid it won't do for the two of us dressed the way we are. Instead I'll bring you to the place that makes the best chow around these parts. All the sailors eat there."

"My father always said sailors know the best food for the best price," I said.

"He was right, he was. Come on, lad!"

"Well, was I right about the food?" Herbie asked.

"You were right. Everything was good. I'm glad I ran into you."

"Me, too. I had a pie-shaped space in my stomach needing to be filled."

"I wasn't sure where to go, or what to do. Is there much action in this town?"

"Plenty! There's a park in town where there's usually a ballgame going on, a band will be playing in the band shell this evening. And of course there's always the beach and swimming."

"I didn't bring my bathing suit, and baseball wasn't the game I had in mind."

"What game were you thinking about?"

"I don't know. What sort of things do you do for fun?" I asked innocently.

"Me? What I do wouldn't be of much interest to a youngster."

"I used to spend time doing things with my father. Sometimes he'd even take me with him when he got together with his friends. You know, they'd talk... and maybe play some cards."

Herbie gave me a questioning look.

"You know... poker and blackjack... sometimes they'd throw dice. Does any of that go on around here?"

"I never heard of a place where it didn't," he answered.

"Do you think you could get me into a game?"

"I could... but I ain't going to."

"Why not?"

"The men at these games are real sharks, and I'm not about to bring a new little fishy for them to gobble down."

"I wouldn't even need to play," I protested. "I just like to watch."

"Nobody just watches a poker game, and I'm not going to just watch you lose all your money. The answer is no."

"Come on, Herbie, I'll find a way to get there with or without you. Wouldn't it be better if you were there to make sure I didn't lose too badly and that nobody took advantage of me?"

He didn't answer right away, which was a good sign. He was really thinking about what I'd said.

"How much money do you have, laddie?"

"Eleven dollars, I mean eleven dollars minus what I have to pay for our bill."

He nodded his head slowly. "Is that your pay for the week?"

I nodded.

"I told you they paid well up there. Tell you what, I always eat my Saturday suppers with the widow Johnson. You think long and hard about this, and if you're still interested I'll meet you right back out front of this place at nine tonight. Okay?"

"You got a deal, and you won't regret it," I said enthusiastically.

"I know I won't regret it, but I'm afraid you might. Then again, you might leave with less money and more wisdom."

I sat on the edge of the sidewalk, kicking up little clouds of dust with my feet. The sun had been down for almost half an hour and it was clearly later than nine o'clock. Anxiously, I'd seen that RCMP officer patrolling the streets. Luckily he'd been occupied with other concerns and hadn't taken notice of me.

My stomach grumbled. I'd only eaten a bite for supper because I wanted to save all my money for gambling.

Now that it looked like Herbie wasn't going to show, everything was closed and there was no place for me to get anything to eat. If I left right now I might still be able to get something back at the house. All day I'd played around with the idea of not going back. Just leaving. There really wasn't any place to go. On the other hand, there really wasn't any reason to stay, either. But not tonight. It was too late.

As I rose to leave I saw Herbie ambling down the street. He was walking with a strange gait and I could hear him singing to himself.

"Was hoping you wouldn't be here," he said in a slurred voice. It was clear he'd done more than eat. I could smell the liquor on his breath. "Do you still want to go?"

I nodded. "I'll be careful."

"No, you won't. If you were careful you'd be home in bed, but come along anyway."

The street was mostly deserted by this time. There were a few couples out strolling arm-in-arm, a group of kids not much different in age from me sitting in front of the general store, and a few men wandering around by themselves. As we passed close by one of the men it was obvious he'd been at the same bottle as Herbie.

We left the street and walked into a dark alleyway, and Herbie started singing to himself again. The farther from the street we got the darker it became, and I moved closer to Herbie, although the idea of this little old man protecting me didn't make much sense.

"Here it is," Herbie said, stopping at the back door of a small building. "Keep close to me, don't bump into anybody and mind your manners. Some of these boys ain't the most polite at the best of times, and they can be downright ornery when they've been drinking and gambling... especially if they're down a few dollars."

He opened the door and I came in beside him. A large man rose to his feet and blocked our way.

"How's she going, Harry?" Herbie called out.

"Who's this?" he asked, pointing at me.

"He's with me, Harry. He's come to learn the fine art of poker from a master."

"The master? You? The only thing you've ever mastered is the bottom of a bottle," Harry taunted him.

"Pure jealousy it is. If it wasn't so dim I'm sure I could see the colour green shining in your eyes."

"Well, I guess he could learn from you."

"That's more like it," Herbie said.

"Learn all the wrong things to do is what I mean. You just watch old Herbie there and do the opposite of whatever he does. How old are you, son? When were you born?" he asked me.

"Shouldn't you want to know how old my money is?" I asked as I pulled it out of my pocket. It wasn't much, but I'd gotten all the bills in ones and had them wrapped around a dozen pieces of paper to make it look like I had a bundle.

Harry chuckled. "I guess any friend of Herbie's is a friend of ours. Come on in and get into a game."

"He's just here to watch!" Herbie protested.

"This isn't a tourist attraction. Either he comes to play or he goes. Got it?"

"Sure, I'll play... as long as somebody can explain the rules to me," I answered, trying to sound as innocent as possible.

"Explain the rules!" he snorted. "I'm sure I can find you a game where people would be willing to teach you a thing or two. Come along."

We followed him along a dimly lit passageway until we came to a door. He knocked three knocks, paused, and knocked three more times. The door swung open.

"We have new players, and I mean really new players," Harry said as he showed us in.

As we entered the room the door closed behind us, with Harry returning to his lookout spot at the back entrance. It was a big room, and while it was a lot brighter than the passageway it was still dim. There were four tables surrounded by men playing cards. Off in one of the corners a half dozen men were crouched down on the ground throwing dice. In the corner three men, one with an accordion and two with fiddles, were playing away loudly. At the back of the room, men stood at a bar throwing back drinks. Judging from the loud conversation, the bottles and glasses present everywhere and the smell in the air, it was clear a lot of liquor was being drunk. This was good for me. The more they drank, the better they'd think they were, and the better I'd do.

"You want a drink?" Herbie asked.

I shook my head. "I don't drink."

"I guess I'll have to drink for the two of us then. Remember what I told you and don't get into any trouble." Herbie wandered over to the bar.

I started to circulate through the room. I needed to investigate the action and decide which game would be best for me to get into. The secret was to check them out without them knowing they were being checked out.

I quickly decided against joining the group playing

dice; they were drunk, which normally would have been good, but the men seemed nasty and bad-natured. There was going to be a fight there sooner or later and I didn't want to be part of it. At the four tables there were men playing poker. Two tables were occupied by players gambling for stakes that were too rich for me. If I got a few unlucky hands to start off then my whole bankroll would be drained off and I'd be finished for the night.

I spent my time watching the two remaining tables. There were six men at one table and five at the other. Both tables were playing straight poker. At one the chips were worth twenty-five cents each, while the other men were playing ten cents a chip.

"Don't stand behind me!" one of the men barked at me.

"Sorry, I was just watching," I apologized.

"Poker isn't a spectator sport. Either play or leave!"

"I'd like to play… but I'm not really sure about all the rules," I replied in a quiet voice.

Suddenly I was aware that eyes at both tables were watching me intently.

"I think we can find a place for him in this game," a man announced.

"No, no, we have an extra spot right here!" somebody from the second table argued, standing and pushing out a chair for me. "You do have money, don't you?"

I pulled my bills from my pocket. The man looked at the money and then practically pulled me down into the seat.

"Does your mama know you're in here tonight, sonny?"

"Nope. She's hundreds of miles away. My friend Herbie brought me."

"Herbie, huh? Well, we've all taken enough of his money so I guess there's no crime in taking a little of his friend's as well. Let's have a new deck for the new player."

The secret of poker is to size the other players up without them being able to size you up. They were playing sloppy poker, and most of the players seemed more interested in keeping track of their drinks than they did in watching the cards. It was soon clear that I was the only person at the table who wasn't at least half in the bag. I let the first few hands pass me by, folding my cards and losing my ante without raising the bet. On the fourth hand I was dealt a pair of aces. I deliberately laughed out loud and then tried to hide my smile as everybody at the table stared at me. I raised the stakes extravagantly and everybody else at the table folded, leaving me with a small pot and, more important, a reputation as a player who couldn't hide a good hand.

"You got good luck, kid. Now if you could just work on that poker face!" one of the men chuckled and the rest laughed along.

"What do you mean?" I asked, feigning ignorance.

"Never you mind. You don't go changing... just keep playing. It's your deal."

"I've got to get going," I said softly.

"It isn't good manners for the winner to be the first to walk away from the table," one of the men scowled.

He and two of his friends had become increasingly unfriendly with every hand I'd won throughout the night. They weren't that much older than me, maybe nineteen or twenty. I hadn't counted my money—it's never a good idea to count your winnings at the table—but I knew I was up almost thirty dollars and the three of them were all down about ten each. They were bad players, and I'd only had to deal off the bottom of the deck a few times and palmed cards no more than half a dozen times during the whole game. The challenge wasn't in beating them but in not beating them too badly or too fast.

"I've got to go. I have to be at work in the morning," I lied.

"You can't just go walking off with our money," a second argued loudly.

"As far as I can tell it isn't your money any more," Harry interrupted from behind me. "You done okay, kid?"

"I guess so."

"He done better than okay. He seemed to win almost all the hands he dealt," the first one, whose name was Angus, argued.

"You down any money?" Harry asked of the older gentleman at our table.

"Maybe two or three dollars."

"And the kid, did he play fair and square?"

"I didn't see anything going on except for plain dumb luck going for him. I'll take luck over skill any day. It was his night, that's all there is to it. I'm going to cash in."

"Maybe everybody should call it a night," Harry suggested.

"Maybe nothing, I'm not leaving without having a chance to get my money back," Angus, the biggest of the men, practically yelled, jumping to his feet.

Suddenly Harry was flanked by three other men, almost all as large as him and considerably larger than Angus.

"I think you better call it a night, friend. If you leave now, all you'll have lost will be a few dollars... start a fight with me and it'll be your teeth you'll be leaving behind," Harry said quietly.

The other two slowly got up and went over to their friend, taking him by the arms. He cursed under his breath and cast me an ugly look but willingly allowed them to lead him away.

"Come on, kid, it's time for you to take your money and run," Harry said.

I gathered up the money in front of me and stuffed it into my pockets. I looked around for Herbie. He was slumped over in a chair in the corner, snoring away loudly.

"Don't worry about Herbie. He sleeps here as often as he does at home. Of course, it might be better if you leave by the front door. No telling what might be waiting in the alley."

I was thinking the same thing myself.

"Come this way," Harry said, cocking a finger.

I followed after him and he led me through a door beside the bar. It led into a darkened shop. We walked down the aisle between rows of canned goods. We were in the general store. I'd been in here earlier in the day getting an ice cream cone. Harry unbolted the front door.

"You don't have to worry about those boys. Once the booze is out of them they'll be fine."

"And while it's still in them?" I asked.

"That's another matter. It looked like Angus was going to try me on for size back there. Thank goodness I didn't have to put him down. I've known him since he was just a lad, and his father before that. You get straight home."

I walked out and heard the door being bolted behind me. The street was completely deserted, and only a couple of streetlights were still burning. I looked anxiously along the length of the street. They were no place to be seen, but there were shadows everywhere that they could be hiding in.

"Good evening."

I jumped and spun around in midair. Corporal O'Malley stepped out of the shadows of a storefront. He walked toward me.

"Did you have yourself a good night?" he asked.

"Umm… yeah… I guess so," I mumbled.

"And did you win or lose?"

I didn't know what to answer so decided to say nothing.

"You look surprised. I already told you last week there isn't anything in this town I don't know about, including where every card game is."

I dug my hands deeper into my pockets and looked down. The light reflected off his shiny boots—boots like I'd seen that night in the arbour. I looked up at him in shock.

"What's wrong, boy? You look like you've seen a ghost."

"No…nothing… I guess I'm just tired. Do you know what time it is?" I asked, trying to divert his attention.

He pulled a watch out of his vest pocket. "The exact time is one-twenty-five. That is well past the time you should be home. I'll expect not to see you again at such an hour. Do you understand my meaning?"

"Yeah."

"Now, get home," he ordered. Before I could even think to respond he turned and walked briskly down the street.

I turned and started to walk in the opposite direction. I walked down the centre of the wide street. I kept swinging my head from side to side, alert for any sign of Angus or his two buddies. As I passed the last darkened house I felt relieved. They were behind me, and there was nothing ahead but a long walk.

It was funny, usually after a night playing cards I kept on thinking about the game, the way the cards were played, the hands I'd played well and those I should have handled differently. Now, I found myself thinking about that hydrofoil and how they didn't want me there, even though I was willing to work for free. Just another place I wasn't wanted.

I turned around suddenly at the sound of feet on the road. There just thirty feet back were two of the men from the game... two of them. I had a terrible feeling that I already knew where the third man was. I turned back around and he was standing in the middle of the road, blocking my way forward. I felt overcome with fear and my body was bathed in a sudden rush of sweat. I looked all around, desperately searching for a way out. The road had narrowed at this point and there was a thicket to one side and a steep drop-off to the other. They'd chosen the spot wisely.

"Don't even think about dropping off the side. It's

forty feet down to the water," one of them yelled. They were closing in on me from both directions.

"Don't do anything stupid, kid. All we want is our money."

"The money you cheated out of us," added the third.

Fighting them wasn't going to work. Two of them were taller than me and all three outweighed me. If I could only get by them there was no way they'd ever catch me. I had to somehow talk my way past them.

"You... you can have your money."

"We know we can have our money!" Angus laughed.

They were now right on top of me. I turned sideways so I could see them coming at me from both sides.

"But we figure we deserve a little more than just our money after what you did ... making us come all this way... cheating us like you did!" Angus growled.

Two of them, one from each side, sprang out at me, grabbing me by both arms. I tried to struggle but they held me firmly. Angus stood directly in front of me with a ugly, sickening smile on his face.

"We're going to take it outta your hide, kid. Teach you to cheat us like you did!"

Chapter Eight

"THIS DOESN'T SEEM LIKE a fair fight to me," came a voice from the shadows at the side of the road.

Held between the two men I turned as best I could toward the voice, as did the three of them. My mouth almost dropped to the ground as Mr. Bell stepped out from among the thick shrubs lining the road. They released me and stepped back. I rubbed one arm, which was stinging badly from where I'd been grabbed so roughly.

"We weren't doing anything—" Angus started to say.

"I know exactly what you were about to do. I'm an old man, but my eyes and ears still work fine," Mr. Bell said.

"We didn't mean any harm, we were just—" Angus began again.

"And how do you figure the three of you whaling away at this lad wouldn't do him any harm? Can you answer that question for me?"

There was no response, but they still looked very angry.

"And there are three of you to the one of him. Is that the way you were raised, to have no sense of fair play? Well, what would your father have to say about that, Angus?"

"My father would say a man should stand up for himself when somebody takes away his money," Angus barked angrily. The other two nodded in agreement.

"And this lad, how did he take your money?" Bell asked.

"In cards. He took our money playing poker," one of the others answered.

"Aye, poker. I thought you barely knew the game, William," Bell said, looking directly at me. He turned back to the men. "And you think that he somehow cheated you, is that correct?"

They all grumbled agreement with his question.

"And how exactly did he cheat you?"

There was more mumbling, but nobody offered an answer right away. I almost laughed. These three hadn't noticed anything.

"Well," Angus said, "we didn't exactly see how he did it, but he must have... we all lost a lot of money."

"I see," Bell said, nodding his head and stroking his beard with one hand. "And did you consider that perhaps you're all just terrible card players?"

"I'm a good player!" Angus protested.

"Well, I've never seen you play, lad, so I suppose I can't disagree... although I have had you working up at Beinn Bhreagh with your father, so I can only assume you're better with cards than you are with a hammer and saw. But never you mind, there's no point in talking any further. You didn't come up for a discussion, did you? Angus, be a good lad and hold my coat for me," he said, as he began to remove his jacket.

"Your coat?" Angus questioned blankly.

"Aye, my coat. This was a present from Mrs. Bell and she'd be most perturbed with me if I got it muddy or ripped. Now it seems that three of you against William is not a fair fight. And even if I were to go on his side you'd still outnumber the two of us by one. So it seems perfectly fair for one of you to hold my coat while the other two fight the two of us."

"You're going to fight us?" one of them asked in confusion.

"Well, not necessarily you two. You could hold my coat and Angus could fight instead. Would that be all right with you, Angus?" Bell asked, turning to Angus.

Angus looked totally confused. "But... but we can't fight you, Mr. Bell."

"Ahhh..." Bell said, nodding his head. "I suppose you have a point. I am probably a bit too old to take part in a roadside brawl, but I have an idea. Angus, since you're the biggest and William is the smallest, it would make sense for the two of you to be on the same side and you can fight the other two. What are your names, lads?"

"Um... I'm Ian."

"And Thomas, sir," the other mumbled.

"Good, excuse me for not stopping for introductions earlier but I'm not up on all the civilities involved in a brawl. All right then, it shall be William and Angus fighting against Thomas and Ian. Angus, hand me back my coat and then you can get things started by taking a poke at Thomas."

"You want me to hit Thomas?" Angus asked. He was now more confused than he was drunk.

"Or Ian. Either one. It doesn't matter which you hit, but I must insist you hit one of them immediately! I haven't the time to be wasting while you discuss the matter!"

"But... but... I can't hit my friends," Angus stammered.

"Either you hit one of them or I'm afraid William and I must leave. It is well past the time I was expected home and I wouldn't want to worry my dear wife." Bell reached over and grabbed me by the arm. "Come William, we must leave."

We walked past Angus and I held my breath as we started off down the road.

"But what about our money?"

Bell stopped and spun around. "Yes, your money. I suggest the three of you go home and sober up. Tomorrow you come by the house and we can talk about your accusations that William cheated you. Perhaps we'll even have to have the corporal over to discuss this. And then, while he's there, we'll discuss this disgusting display I witnessed here tonight!" Bell threatened. His voice had become loud and deep and angry. He stepped back toward the three men and raised his walking stick in front of him.

"Now be gone with you before I make up my mind to take my stick and give the three of you a sound thrashing!"

I felt my heart rise up into my throat and then almost instantly settle back into place as the three of them put their tails between their legs and scurried away toward town without saying a word. Bell chuckled softly to himself as they vanished into the darkness.

"Come, lad."

I fell into step beside him. He was setting a tremendous pace and I struggled to keep up. I was grateful for the darkness that enveloped us.

"Mr. Bell?"

"Yes, William?"

"I… I was just wondering…"

"How I happened to be at that spot at this time?"

"Yes."

"I was out for my evening stroll when I heard a commotion coming through the trees. I was curious so I went to investigate."

"And that's when you saw us."

"Oh no, you were no place to be seen when I first came upon those three. I followed behind them for a while, and when they stopped I took up a position where I could observe. I knew something of interest would be occurring. They certainly captured your interest, didn't they, William?"

I didn't know what to say in response. I was struggling to keep up with his fast, lanky strides. I was amazed at how quickly he was moving.

"Hardly anything better than a long walk… at night…

through the forest or by the water... alone to think. It just cleans the mind of all the things that accumulate during the day. Allows for new thoughts and ideas, or a new way of looking at old thoughts and ideas. It's an almost perfect night. Shame it isn't raining."

"You want it to be raining?"

"Aye. The water washing down just cleanses the mind. I imagine it seems pretty peculiar, an old man walking in the rain in the wee hours of the night. Some people might think it was batty, don't you think?" he asked. There was a hint of a smile hidden beneath his thick beard and lost in the moonlight.

"It's late. Luckily it's Sunday so you'll have no responsibilities for the day and can sleep in."

"I had offered to get up early and help with some work," I said. I wanted him to think that maybe I wasn't as worthless as he'd probably heard.

"On your day off?" he asked in an astonished tone.

"It's with Casey... Mr. Baldwin... at the boathouse."

"Ahh. That would explain it. Fascinating thing that hydrofoil is . . . but of course you know that isn't possible."

"That's what he said."

"It's just too dangerous, lad."

I didn't need to hear the same sorry excuses.

We fell back into an uneasy silence. The only sounds were our feet against the gravel and the background rumble of the waves hitting against the shoreline.

"Come through here," Bell said. He'd stopped walking and held back a large branch of a bush. "This is a shortcut."

I pushed between the bushes and a branch whacked me in the forehead. I put up my hands to protect my face and continued to wade through the thick undergrowth. I trudged after him, and just as I was beginning to think we were never going to reach the end of the "shortcut" I popped through the brush and found myself standing in a field.

"Do you know where you are?" Bell asked.

It didn't look familiar. I knew we were probably on the grounds of the estate but I couldn't pick enough landmarks out of the gloom to pinpoint the location.

"Sheepville is just over the meadow and the orchard is behind the..." He stopped, and the expression on his face looked deadly serious.

For an instant I was hit with the thought that Angus and his two friends were back.

"What's wrong?"

"Shhhh!" he hissed.

I fell into an uneasy and confused silence.

"Do you smell it?"

"Smell what?" I asked, but then I inhaled deeply and knew what it was. "Smoke... I can smell smoke."

Bell bent down and pulled out a handful of grass. He tossed it into the air and the blades flickered back down to earth and toward us.

"I thought as much. The wind is blowing into our faces. Come on, lad, we have to hurry!"

I rushed to catch up with him. He was moving at a tremendous clip.

"Maybe it's just a fireplace, or somebody burning leaves."

"In July?"

"Or rubbish," I suggested in desperation.

"Not at two o'clock in the morning. Save your breath for walking."

We rounded the edge of the woods and Bell skidded to a stop. There before us was the boathouse, and a thin column of smoke was rising from it.

Chapter Nine

A FLICKERING OF LIGHT was visible through the window of the side door.

"Should I run to the house for help?" I gasped.

"No time. Before anybody could get back it would be too late… if it isn't too late already."

We hurried to the building. Bell held out a hand. "Stop here, lad. You're to come no closer."

He rushed over to the side door and peered in through the glass. When he moved around the corner of the building to the front I circled around after him. He stopped by the large sliding door and I could see him struggling to unhook the bolt that held the door in place. All at once the bolt came up and he slid the door open. Smoke billowed out through the opening and up into the sky. Bell cringed and fell backwards onto the grass. I rushed forward and could feel the heat from the fire against my face.

"Mr. Bell, are you all right?" I yelled as I crouched down beside him.

"Get back! Get away from the building. Go to the house and get help!"

"But you said there wasn't time to get help."

"Don't listen to what I said, listen to what I'm saying!" he bellowed. He stood up and pulled me to my feet. The whole top half of the door way was hidden by smoke, and fire was visible in the far corner of the building.

"What are you going to do?"

"That's not your concern! Now do as you have been told!" he snapped. Then he spun me around by the shoulders and pushed me off away from the building.

I started running on an diagonal away from the boathouse. I looked back as I ran and saw Bell's outline silhouetted against the fire's light. Suddenly he dropped to his knees. He crawled beneath the billowing smoke and disappeared inside the building. My head reeled and I skidded to a stop. What was he doing? Had he lost his mind?

I turned around and raced back. The heat from the fire was already intense and I dropped to my knees as I neared the building. I tried to peer inside but the smoke was much thicker; it now filled the top of the building extending, down to a few feet above the ground. My hand brushed against one of the tracks leading from the water and into the blazing building. I edged forward, sliding my hand along the rail. As long as I kept hold of the track I could find my way in, and even more important back out again. Then like a shot in the head, I realized what I was telling myself—I was going into the burning building after him. I moved forward until I was just on the edge of the entrance. I looked back along the metal track, sloping down and away from the building until it entered the water. I wished I could run down and soak myself before going inside but I knew there wasn't time. I crawled over one rail so I was in the middle of the tracks. Somehow, locked between the two rails I couldn't possibly get lost or be in danger. I took a deep breath of clean, cool, fresh air and pushed forward, breaking the invisible barrier, and crawled into the building.

The smoke was even more intense but I pushed myself forward. My left arm buckled and I fell flat on my face. I lifted my head and peered all around. The fire was raging in the far corner, around the workbenches and the storage area. It was growing quickly and tongues of flame spread out in all directions. The sound of the fire was overwhelming and filled my ears. The HD-4 was only a dozen feet ahead of me on the tracks. It was almost completely veiled in smoke but apparently it had been spared from the flames so far. I pressed forward until I was right at the bow of the ship.

"William, what are you doing?"

My eyes opened wide. Bell was no more than three feet in front of me. He was leaning against the ladder leading up to the hydrofoil. I stumbled over the rail to his side.

"Mr. Bell, we have to—"

An explosion filled the air and forced the words from my throat.

"Get up! Climb up the ladder!" Bell yelled over the roar of the fire.

"What?"

"The ladder, the ladder! Climb up the ladder and get into the cockpit of the boat!"

I remained motionless but my eyes followed the rungs of the ladder up and into the smoke. He couldn't be serious.

"The whole place could explode at any second! Take a deep breath and climb the ladder! There isn't time to waste!" he screamed into my ear.

Still I didn't move.

"I'll be right behind you!" He shoved me and I started up the ladder.

Just short of the veil of smoke I took a deep breath and hurried up the next step. The smoke was thick and filled my nostrils and stung my eyes. I scrambled over the edge of the boat and fell heavily into the cockpit, landing on my back. The smoke was far less thick and I took another breath. Looking up through the smoke I saw bright red fingers of flame flash across the ceiling.

"Ugghhh!" I screamed as Bell tumbled on top of me. Our arms and legs were intertwined and his knees and elbows dug into me painfully as he rolled over and took to his knees.

"The release—we have to push the release!"

He put both hands against a lever and I could see the strain in his face, illuminated more clearly by a sudden burst of flames that pressed me back against the floor of the hydrofoil.

"It's stuck! I can't move it. Help, William, put your weight into it!"

I rolled over and wormed my way forward on my belly.

"The lever! The lever! Pull it!"

I rose to my knees and pulled the lever while Bell pushed against it from the opposite direction. It rocked slightly back and forth with our efforts but remained firmly locked in place.

There were two more explosions in rapid succession and I felt something splatter against my face. Almost instantly the ceiling burst into one patch of brilliant red and a surge of heat smashed me in the face. Suddenly the lever cracked and Bell fell forward, while I tumbled backward. I put my hands over my face to shield my eyes from the blazing flames. The heat and smoke pressed down, and I knew I was helpless to escape. My head felt like it was spinning... and then... at first slowly, and then faster... we were moving. The smoke disappeared and the night sky appeared above my head. I just lay there on my back and watched as the roar of the fire faded, the cool night air surrounded me, and the stars twinkled brightly. We were rolling along the gentle incline toward the water, picking up speed. There was a bump and tremendous splash and a few drops of water hit my face.

I heard soft laughter, Bell's laughter, and pushed myself up. He was lying there, propped up on his elbow. He rose to a sitting position and I did likewise. Side by side we looked over the side of the hydrofoil at the boathouse. Smoke poured out of every window and door and flames shot through the roof and reached up into the sky, throwing sparks up to the heavens. Repeated explosions flashed out even brighter and the sound cannoned down the slope.

"What do you have all over you, William?"

"What?" I turned to Bell and saw blue and green streaks covering his face and beard and hair. I looked at my hands and realized they were covered too.

"Paint. It must be paint," he said, answering his own question. "The explosions are cans of paint. We must have been splattered when one of them exploded."

The hydrofoil rocked gently, and I could tell we were drifting slowly away from shore.

"Shouldn't we do something?" I asked

"There isn't much for us to do. Surely they'll now be able to notice the fire at the house and people will come to investigate. Somebody will tow us back to land."

He started chuckling and chortling to himself, at first softly and then much louder.

"Are you all right, Mr. Bell?" I asked, wondering if the heat or fire had got to him, or maybe one of the exploding paint containers had hit him in the head.

"I'm fine, lad, just fine. It's just... lately I've been feeling old... but not tonight. Just think, in one night I almost got into a fight with three young hooligans, then ran into a burning building and saved the HD-4. This has been a most eventful and exciting evening. Most exciting. I feel younger tonight than I have in many a year!"

Chapter Ten

I SAT BOLT UPRIGHT IN bed and the previous night's events flashed through my mind. It couldn't have been real, it couldn't... I looked down at my legs. I'd gone to bed in my clothes, in spite of the dried paint, and my pants were still streaked with lines and blotches of bright red and green. I got to my feet and undid the buttons of my shirt, which was similarly stained. Pulling it off produced the strong scent of smoke. I removed my pants as well and replaced them with fresh clothing from my drawer. Then once I'd finished dressing, I quickly ran down the noisy steps and into the morning sunlight. I wasn't sure of the time, but judging from how low the sun was in the sky, it was still early morning.

I was racked by a coughing fit and stopped. Gagging, I spat up a large lump of black goop onto the grass. I knew this was some of the smoke and stuff

I'd inhaled during the fire. Last night, well after we'd left the scene of the blaze, little puffs of smoke were still coming out of my mouth when I coughed. I took a deep breath and could almost feel my lungs expanding.

I hadn't been able to get to sleep for a long time after finally reaching my bed. The events of the night kept going around and around in my head, and I couldn't shut my mind down. Mr. Bell had told me that some of the materials in the boathouse were so flammable they would have produced an incredibly hot fire; so hot that if we hadn't got out they never would have known for certain what had happened to us, because even our bones would have melted or burned to ash. I flexed the fingers on one hand and held them up. It was good to still have my bones where they belonged.

Within a few minutes of us hitting the water, the first people had noticed the fire and come running through the night. We'd heard their cries well before we could see them. At first they hadn't even noticed us floating in the darkness offshore in the hydrofoil. We screamed and yelled to get their attention. Mr. Bell's fear was that somebody was going to get hurt trying to put out what was a hopelessly out-of-control fire.

"Only a fool would run into a burning building," he said to me, and began chuckling to himself.

When they noticed us, a rowboat was put out. A line was tied to the HD-4 and we were towed back to shore. Mr. Bell had everybody stand well back from the building, and in time it seemed like every single person on the estate, including Mrs. Bell herself, was gathered in a semicircle watching the inferno. And it was well worth watching.

Aside from the flames, there were regular explosions and towers of fire bursting up into the night sky. Sometimes the flames were tinted with different colours, as barrels or canisters or cans of paint and varnish were consumed. It was like the fireworks displays they had in Halifax harbour to celebrate Queen Victoria's birthday, only better.

Most of the staff were still standing around watching when Mrs. Bell, having noticed the paint and soot covering Mr. Bell and me, insisted we come back to the house and get "looked at" and "cleaned up." She was very kind to me, and she tried to be gentle with the varsol when she was rubbing the paint off my face, but she was less than kind with her husband. She called him an "old fool" for going into the building and asked him how he'd feel if some "idiot" had led one of his grandchildren into a burning building, and I could tell she was really scouring at his skin to remove the paint. Mr. Bell didn't argue with anything, he just kept saying "yes, dear" or "no, dear," and he tried to look like he was sorry, but a couple of times when she wasn't looking he winked at me and I could swear I saw laughter in his eyes.

My stomach grumbled and I started thinking I should head for breakfast. But my curiosity was crying even louder than my hunger, so I went toward the remains of the boathouse rather than the kitchen.

Thin wisps of smoke rose up from behind the trees. I doubled my pace, and as I rounded the edge of the forest I could see the building, or I guess really the charred shell of it. There were three men standing off to the side; getting closer, I recognized Casey and the two Stewarts. They were huddled together, obviously deep in discussion. For the most part, the building had been reduced to a pile of smouldering white ashes. Pieces of charred metal, cans and barrels, beams and struts poked out at awkward angles. Some had taken strange new shapes, having been melted in the furnace of the fire and then cooled. Resting out in the lake, the HD-4 bobbed gently on the waves. It was anchored to the tracks by two lines and looked as though it were peacefully sleeping after the difficult night.

"Billy, how are you feeling?" Casey asked.

I was startled. "Okay, I guess. I can still feel it a bit in my chest. How is Mr. Bell?"

"Oh, fine, I imagine. He seemed fine at bedtime. Of course, we won't get an update until he gets up," Casey said. He looked at his watch. "And that won't be for another four or five hours at least. He never gets up early, and after a night like last night it'll be well past noon before they even attempt to pry his eyes open. By the way, I wanted to thank you."

"Thank me?"

"For saving the hydrofoil," he answered, motioning to the craft.

"It was Mr. Bell who did everything."

"That's not what I heard. Before Mrs. Bell hauled the two of you away last night, Alec told me if it hadn't been for you there wouldn't be an HD-4."

"I just did what Mr. Bell ordered me to do."

"Not likely. I can't see Alec ordering you or anybody else to risk his life. That was something you did on your own, and I'm grateful."

"I just wish we could have put out the fire and saved the boathouse."

"The boathouse isn't important. Everything of value is out there," he said, gesturing toward the HD-4 gently rocking on the waves, "locked away here," he continued, tapping his head, "or, most important, sound asleep with the blinds drawn at the main house. All we've lost in the fire is some materials and parts. This will hardly set us back a hiccup."

Casey's voice was cut off by the sound of an engine and grinding gears. A large truck appeared, rumbling along the path leading up to the boathouse.

"You still want to offer your help this morning?" Casey asked.

"Help with what?"

"The hydrofoil, of course."

"But... but... how...?"

"We need more help than ever," old Mr. Stewart said, "if we hope to rebuild the boathouse before nightfall."

The truck screeched to a stop and two men jumped out of the back.

"Everything we'll need is in the back of the truck. We're going to rebuild it a little better, a little bigger and a little bit closer to the water."

"And perhaps most important, with a separate building off to the side to store the flammables. We won't be making the same mistake again."

People trickled in from the staff house and from town until there were more than three dozen of us working. I was really shaken when I saw Angus wielding a hammer and nails. He nodded at me but didn't say a thing about the previous night. Either he'd been too drunk to remember what had occurred, or he remembered but was too embarrassed to say anything. Everybody worked under the direction of old Mr. Stewart, and things went smoothly. While we worked, pots of coffee and freshly baked muffins and bread, slathered with fresh butter, were brought up to us from the kitchen. By noon the skeleton of the building was in place. Lunch was also brought up to the site, and we shovelled down heaping bowls of stew between hammer blows and saw cuts. Mrs. McCauley-Brown supervised the distribution of the meal. She gave me a big hug and a kiss along with my stew and bread.

The ashes of the old building, which had had water poured on them and were no longer smoking, were visible through the framing of the back wall. My attention was caught by the sight of Mr. Bell, standing over the remains of the boathouse. He was poking at it with a broom handle. I tucked my hammer in my tool belt and went over to see what he was doing.

A pile of objects, mainly pieces of metal, lay at his feet. As I watched, he continued to fish more items out of the ashes. He was talking to himself quietly and I couldn't hear what he was saying. I cleared my throat loudly and he looked up at me.

"You came to work, did you?"

I nodded. "I've been here for a while. What are you looking for?"

"I have no idea. Most likely nothing, but possibly something. Many, many inventions and discoveries have been made by accident. I was wondering if this accident might reveal something wondrous and unique."

I looked down at the objects he'd piled on the ground.

He smiled. "And thus far this accident has produced nothing of value."

"What do you think caused the fire?" I asked.

"I'm not sure. There could be a number of possible causes."

It wasn't unusual to hear the horsedrawn fire wagons going by in Halifax. Houses and stores and warehouses often burned down. Usually it was caused by cooking, or somebody not being careful with their cigarettes or a buildup of gunk in the chimney that sparked a fire on the roof.

"I suspect it was probably spontaneous combustion."

"Spontaneous…?"

"Combustion. The fumes from certain substances, like those used to seal the hull of the HD-4, can burst into flames all by themselves if they are improperly stored or cleaned. I can think of no other reason."

I was happy to hear he had a reason. I'd been going over and over it in my mind and couldn't think of any way this fire could have happened except one: somebody had deliberately set it. Even stranger, and I had no reason to explain why I was even thinking it, I wondered if that meeting I'd witnessed in the arbour had something to do with it.

"I saw young Angus working. Did he ask you for his money back?"

"No," I answered, shaking my head. I felt embarrassed talking about it. "He hasn't said a word to me."

"That doesn't surprise me. He's not a bad lad. Probably wants to just forget the whole thing happened." He paused. "I guess he's not alone in that respect, is he?"

He was right about that.

"And here, take this," he said, handing me an envelope.

I held it in my hand. It was made from a special expensive parchment and it had my name on the front written in a beautiful, flowing script. The dirt from my hands marked the envelope.

"I think the secret is to open it," Bell teased me.

"What?" I asked in confusion, still holding the envelope. "Oh, yeah, open it."

I turned it over. It wasn't sealed. I removed a piece of paper and unfolded it.

Dear William,

The hour was late last night and I did not have the opportunity to thank you more formally for your gallant and brave efforts in helping to save the HD-4, but more important in being there with my husband. He is neither as young nor as handsome as when I first laid eyes upon him, but somehow I find myself still deeply in love with him, and thank you for helping to keep him from harm. I would be honoured if you would join us for dinner tonight.

With affection,
Mrs. Alexander Graham Bell

I looked up at Mr. Bell, who was looking directly at me.

"I do hope you'll be able to join us."

"Yeah, I guess I can," I stammered.

"Good! It appears that Mrs. Bell has taken a shine to you. I think it's hard on the dear girl without the grandchildren around this summer. Dinner is served at seven o'clock. I think you should join us an hour before that."

I knew we wouldn't be through working by then. There'd already been talk of hooking up extra lights so we could continue to work past sunset.

"Then maybe I can't come tonight," I apologized.

"But why?"

"I need to stay and help if they're going to work late."

"It's admirable that you feel that way, but I must insist. We have to discuss some changes in your employment."

"Changes?" I asked, and a lump formed in my throat.

"Yes. Mr. McGregor and I were speaking."

This didn't sound like good news. I knew he'd been told of the complaints about my work. I was going to get fired, and after all that I'd done the night before... but that was just plain stupid. He wasn't going to discharge me. Although he might give me a lecture, I thought.

"So I will expect you at six, unless you have further objections."

"No, no, I'll be..." I paused and slowed myself down. "Yeah, I guess that would be okay."

"Excellent! I'll tell Mr. Stewart you are to finish up at four this afternoon. That will give you time to clean up and arrive before dinner."

Chapter Eleven

"GOOD TO SEE YOU, WILLIAM. Please come in and have a seat," Mr. Bell said, gesturing toward a chair.

He was sitting at a big desk in his study, holding a pen in one hand and a lit cigar in the other. Smoke swirled up and into a small cloud pinned against the ceiling.

"These things haven't tasted so good today," he said, waving the cigar. "Handmade from the finest Cuban tobacco… very expensive. Very hard to get. I cherish each and every one."

He knew about the three missing cigars.

"You don't smoke, do you?"

"Um… no," I lied.

"I didn't think so. Very wise. Smoking is a bad habit. One of many that people become absorbed by. So tell me, how long have you been playing poker?"

"Not long," I answered truthfully. It was only in the past year that I'd really learned how to play the game.

"Then I was right."

"Right about what?"

"You must be a very smart young man to become so good in only a short time."

"I'm not that good," I replied. I made a point of keeping my head up and continuing to look at him. The most believable way to lie is to look somebody square in the eyes.

"Don't hide your light under a bushel, William."

"What?" I asked.

"It means there's nothing wrong with letting somebody know you're good at something."

Obviously he knew nothing about poker.

"I'm not talking about being a braggart or anything," he continued. "Nothing is more annoying than somebody who's full of himself. I'm just saying you should take credit for your accomplishments."

"But I'm really not that good," I persisted.

"I must disagree. I can't speak for all three of those young men the other night, but I know that Angus is not stupid, nor was he very drunk, so you must be a very good player to have taken his money."

He was partially right. I was a good player, but those three really were stupid and drunk.

"And of course I watched you that first night when you were observing the bridge game. You were so busy looking at the cards that you didn't notice me looking at you, did you?"

I hated to admit it, even to myself, but he was right. All my attention had been riveted on the cards.

"You were studying the game, and I could tell you quickly understood not just its rules but its subtle play. I was particularly amused by the small changes in your expression when people played wrong or questionable cards."

I was shocked that he could have read me that way. I tried to keep my expression completely neutral now so that he would be unable to judge my reaction.

"There, now that's much better! You just put on a ... what do they call it? ... a poker face. Excellent!" he thundered. "And don't worry, I'm sure nobody else at the bridge game, with the exception of my wife, even noticed. The deaf, and people who work with the deaf, learn to read people's facial expressions with much more accuracy than others."

"You work with the deaf?" I asked meekly.

"Oh, good gracious! I think I shall be remembered as the inventor of the telephone, but that was just an invention, one of thousands that came before it and many more thousands that will follow. Working with the deaf is the most important thing I've ever done. I am, above all else, a teacher." He paused. "Being a teacher is one of, if not *the* noblest of professions. Have you ever considered becoming a teacher?"

"No, I've never thought of that."

"What vocation does interest you?"

"I really haven't given it much thought."

"There is still time for you to find your calling, although

it is never too early. I would suggest it should be some field in which mathematics is important. You're good at mathematics and calculation."

How could he know that?

"Don't look so surprised. Bridge, and I suspect poker as well, is a very mathematical game. You must constantly do mental arithmetic, calculate probabilities and odds. Very taxing mathematics." He paused. "Say, do you think you could do me a favour?"

It was now my turn to pause. "I... I guess I could."

"Excellent. I was hoping you could become my teacher."

"Your teacher? What could I teach you?" I asked in astonishment.

"Poker."

"You want me to teach you poker?"

"Yes, I've heard that many people enjoy it."

"But I'm really not very good," I asserted once again.

"Fine, we'll agree you're really not that good. But you know, in the country of the blind, the one-eyed man is king."

"Huh?" What was he talking about now?

"It means that even if you are not very good you still know much more than me, and can teach me. Unless of course you think I'm so old and daft that I couldn't possible learn the game?"

"No, no, of course not—"

"Good!" he interrupted. "Then it is settled! Come and you shall teach me to play poker."

He ground out the stub of his cigar in the ashtray, rose

to his feet and walked out of the room. "Come on, William, we must find a place to play!" he bellowed over his shoulder, and I quickly trotted after him. He moved with the same long, lanky gait that had propelled him along the road the night before, and I couldn't catch him before he had disappeared into another room. I hesitated and then entered after him. It was a room off to the side of the house. It was a little library filled with books and comfortable chairs for reading. A large bay window dominated one wall and brilliant sunlight still shone in through the glass.

"Do we need a special table or will this one do?" he asked of a rectangular wooden table that was partway into the alcove formed by the bay window.

"This one will be fine."

"Good. Have a seat and I'll go and get a package of cards," Bell said as he retreated out of the room.

I walked over to the table and ran my hand along the smooth, gleaming wooden top. There were four chairs around the table and I selected my seat, the chair that was backing into the bay window. It was a trick I'd been taught: if you sit with brilliant light gleaming in behind you, your opponent has to avert his eyes and can't read your expression.

"Here we go, a new package. Will you open it up and shuffle the deck?"

I followed his directions.

"Please proceed, and teach me the game," he said.

"Do you know anything about poker at all?"

"A little. We get to trade these cards for others if we don't like them, right?"

"Up to four of your cards can be discarded."

"That seems very sporting. And what makes a good or winning hand?"

"The highest combinations. Two of a kind is better than an ace—"

"Two of a kind?"

"Yeah, like a pair of fives or two queens."

"And two queens would be more than two jacks but less valuable than two kings?"

"Exactly. But two of anything isn't as good as three of a kind. So three twos is better than two aces."

He nodded enthusiastically. "And four aces would be the best you could get and would beat anything!"

"It would be good, but it wouldn't beat the best hand. Let me explain about straights and a royal flush and—"

"Enough talk. You learn only part of what you're told, most of what you're shown and all of what you do. Deal."

I shuffled the deck.

"How many do we each get?" Mr. Bell asked.

"Mostly five cards."

"Mostly?"

"Well there are seven-card games, but in straight poker it's just five," I explained.

"I think we should start with five. Seven cards would just make it more complicated. Let's keep it simple."

I started dealing the cards. Mr. Bell picked up his as they slid across the table. He held them very sloppily and I caught a flash of an ace of hearts. This was going to be interesting.

We played six hands. He discarded almost all his cards

each deal but luck was with him and he actually won twice. Out of habit I dealt off the bottom of the deck when I was dealing one hand.

"This certainly is a boring game," Mr. Bell proclaimed.

"Well, it's different when there are more people and betting."

"There's no one else around to play, but we could wager if that would add more interest to the game."

I looked up at him. Was he serious?

"I know, I know, you're probably feeling bad about taking my money."

That wasn't what I was thinking at all. He was being pretty nice to me and everything, but I'd seen people get pretty nasty when they lose money, like the other night, and I couldn't really afford for my boss to be angry with me.

"But I wouldn't object. It would be like paying you for teaching me the game. And besides, I might even end up taking some of your money," he chuckled. "You do have some money with you, don't you?"

"Yes… some," I answered. Actually I had every cent I owned on me. Some was in the wallet I carried in my front pocket while most of it was safely rolled away in a money belt I wore under my clothing.

"Excellent! Excuse me while I go and get some money. We keep fairly large sums in the house to pay wages for the staff and expenses, but I very seldom have any on me."

He rose and once again left the room, this time going through a set of big double doors that led into his study. He quickly returned. He was carrying a metal box which he put down noisily on the table. He flipped open the lid, reached in and pulled out a small pile of bills, putting them down on the table beside the box. I could tell there was at least twenty or thirty dollars there, and I couldn't help but wonder how much more was hidden away inside. I moved slightly in my seat and craned my neck to try and look over the edge of the box, and almost in answer he closed the lid and put the box down under the table and out of sight.

"Now what do we do?" he asked.

"Ante up. We start the game by putting money in the centre. That's the pot we're trying to win."

"Ahh, yes, this does add something to it right away. How much shall I put in?" Mr. Bell asked as he fanned the bills.

"It depends. Sometimes a nickel or a dime or—"

"How about a dollar? It would make it so much easier, and I think the sound of coins hitting against the table would be most annoying."

I loved the sound of coins or poker chips bouncing off a table. The only thing nicer was the scraping sound they made when you won a pot and were pulling them across the table toward you.

"I guess we could put a dollar in."

It was my turn to deal. I shuffled the deck and offered it to Mr. Bell to cut. He declined, the way he had every time. The challenge here wasn't whether I was going to win but to not win too much. I set a figure of fifteen dollars in winnings as the amount I'd limit myself to. I wouldn't take any more of his money than that.

Mr. Bell discarded four of his five cards and I dealt

him the replacements. He took them into his hands, and there was a subtle change in his expression that led me to believe he was pleased by the new cards. I discarded two. I kept a pair of sevens and a king. My two new cards were useless.

"This is where I can bet more money if I think I can beat you, right?"

"It's called raising."

"Okay." He reached down to his money and counted out five bills. He set them down in the pot. "Ten dollars."

"You want to bet ten dollars?" I questioned.

"Is that too much?" he asked innocently.

"Well, I guess it depends on whether or not you think you have a good hand."

"Oh… oh… can I change my bet?"

"Not in a real game, but you can if you want because you're learning," I offered.

"Thank you." He reached over, plucked another bill off his pile and threw it into the pot. "Make it fifteen dollars."

I shook my head and put down my cards. "I fold."

"Fold?"

"That means I give up. You win the hand."

"Excellent! I win!" he trumpeted loudly. He put his cards on the table. He had a pair of threes. I would have won!

He raked in the pot, including my dollar. "And you were right, wagering has added a whole new level of interest to this game! I'll try not to win too much of your money," Bell chuckled, and I felt the hackles on my back rise up.

I nodded politely but could feel my temper rising. I'd just see how he felt about it when he was on the losing end.

The second hand went the same way as the first; he won my dollar by scaring me out of the game with a big raise. Either he was bluffing or he just didn't know any better and was going to bet on anything. I shuffled the deck thoroughly. He was looking off, away from me toward the open door at the side of the room. I quickly noted the bottom three cards so I could deal them to myself later if they were needed.

Once again he declined to cut and I dealt the cards. He looked at each card as it came; he grimaced three times and put those cards on the left-hand side while two other cards were received more favorably and put on the right of the others. This was one of the tricks to look for: players often put their good cards on one side of their hand and their bad ones on the other. He discarded the three cards from the left side of his hand. I had to fight to keep my smile hidden. He then raised the pot by ten dollars. My cards were good and I saw his raise and threw another dollar in. Mr. Bell chuckled and then met my raise and called. I placed my cards on the table; I had three jacks. His smile evaporated. He silently put his cards down, gathered the deck and started shuffling.

He wasn't happy, but I was pretty pleased to have some of his money sitting in my pile. Maybe I could raise the limit I was going to win. After all, he'd hardly miss the money, and I was going to give him a *real lesson*.

We played for over an hour. He won an occasional hand but I was winning more than three out of four. Even more important, when I did lose I lost only a few dollars, and when I won I was getting a big return. I hadn't counted my winnings, but I knew I was up by more than forty dollars. At one point, Mrs. McCauley-Brown came to summon us for dinner, but Mr. Bell said we'd be eating later and the rest should eat without us.

He continued to telegraph his cards—a little gleam in his eyes when a good one came, putting the bad ones off to the left side, betting too quickly and too big when he really had nothing in his hand. Maybe he was right and you can't teach an old dog new tricks. And to think I was worried that he'd be able to "read me" too easily.

There was also starting to be a desperation to his play. The more he was getting down, the less careful and considered his bets were becoming. I knew if I wanted I could walk out of that room with hundreds of dollars.

Mr. Bell shuffled the cards, let me cut and then dealt. I picked up my cards but kept my eyes trained on him as he picked up his cards and studied them. Four of the cards were greeted by a small grimace and placed to the left of his hand while the fifth was met with a blank expression. Satisfied, I looked at my cards: three nines and two sevens, a full house!

"Cards, William?"

"I'll play the ones I was dealt."

"Hah! They can't all be that good. You must be bluffing. I'll take... oh... three... no, make that four," he said dealing himself replacements.

I studied his reaction. Three of the four cards were given a bad response while the fourth was put over to the far right side of his hand. That meant that the very most he could possibly have would be a pair, and the highest pair was a pair of aces. Obviously he had nothing to match my full house.

"Well, William, we should be getting to dinner. Why don't we make this the last hand?"

"That's all right with me."

"Good." He paused. He seemed to be gazing out the door and into the distance. "I think I'll raise thirty-five dollars," he said as he counted off the money and threw it in the pot.

"Thirty-five dollars!" I exclaimed.

"Did I say thirty-five? I meant forty-five," he said, and added a ten-dollar bill to the pile.

I hesitated. I knew my hand was better than his, but if I won I'd be well above the limit I'd set for myself.

"Come on, William, don't be such an old woman," he taunted. "You know what they say, if you can't stand the heat you'd better get out of the kitchen."

I chuckled. "I can stand the heat. Maybe I just don't want to take too much of your money."

"Don't worry about me. Worry about yourself."

"Fine. I'll see your raise and raise you another ten dollars," I responded.

"I hear your voice but I don't see your money. This game isn't played on credit. As I understand it, either you have the money or you fold."

"I have the money," I said defiantly. I rose from the table and lifted up my shirt to reveal my money belt.

"So that's where you keep your wealth. Do you have enough to match my bet?"

"More than match," I snapped. I unbuttoned the belt

and took out the bills. I counted out fifty-five dollars and laid it on the table.

"Doesn't leave you with much, does it?" he asked.

"If I lose… but I'm not going to lose."

Bell laughed loudly. "It's good to be confident… at least good for *me* that you're confident. Well, William, I'm going to see your raise," he said, putting ten more dollars in the pot, "and I'm going to raise you another hundred dollars."

"A hundred dollars!"

"Yes."

"But that isn't fair!" I protested.

"There's nothing unfair about it." He reached under the table and grabbed the box. He opened it and removed a stack of bills. He quickly counted out the money and threw it into the pot. "Are you going to see my raise?"

"I can't see your raise. I haven't got enough money!"

"I guess I win," he said as he reached out and put his hands on the pot to rake it in. He stopped and looked directly up at me. "Unless…" He stopped.

"Unless what?" I asked anxiously.

"What are your wages per week?"

"Eleven dollars."

"And you're working here for another ten weeks, so that is one hundred and ten dollars. I could give you your summer's salary in advance."

"You'd lend me the money?"

"Well… I probably shouldn't. It wouldn't be right for me to take your entire summer's earnings. Let's just forget that idea," Bell said, and he started pulling the money toward him.

"Wait! Just lend me the money!" I pleaded.

"For you to match my bet?"

"Yes."

"I've heard them say you shouldn't gamble if you can't afford to lose. I can afford to lose, but can you?"

I didn't answer. There was no gamble involved here. I knew I had the better hand. "So can I have the money?"

He hesitated for just a second and then counted out the bills. He pushed them toward me. I reached out to take them and he put his hand on top of mine.

"If I win, you know you have no choice but to work here all summer for absolutely no money. Understand?"

I nodded.

He removed his hand and I moved the money halfway across the table, leaving it in the pot in the centre of the table.

"And I raise you another seven dollars," I said, taking my last few dollars and throwing them onto the pile.

A smile crossed his face. "Do you really think I'll fold for seven more dollars, William? Not likely!" He matched my few dollars. "Well, William, let's see your cards."

I put down the pair of sevens.

"That's it! You bet all of this money on just a pair! You don't think I can beat a pair of sevens?" he thundered.

I then put down the trio of nines. "And three nines. Full house." I reached forward and grabbed for the pot.

"Don't you think you should wait to see my cards?"

I stopped but didn't remove my hands.

He turned over the cards one by one and placed them down on the table in front of him: ace of hearts… king of hearts… queen of hearts… jack of hearts.

My heart had risen farther up my throat with each card. If the last card he was holding was the ten of hearts, then I had lost… not just the game but my whole summer. But it couldn't possibly be that card. Nobody could draw four cards to complete a royal flush.

Almost in slow motion he took the card and laid it down on the table beside the other four. The ten of hearts.

Chapter Twelve

I FELT LIKE I'D BEEN kicked in the stomach. Slowly, trembling, I withdrew my hands.

Suddenly Mr. Bell leapt to his feet. He started dancing around the table like an Indian circling a campfire. I jumped as he let out an ear-piercing whoop. If I could have, I would have run out of the room, but my legs were shaking so badly I didn't think they'd carry me. He plopped back down in his chair and raked in the money.

"That was a genuine war dance. Taught to me by members of the Mohawk Indian tribe. I'm an honorary member."

I took a deep breath.

"You were right, William. Poker can be a very interesting game. It's sad for you, though, that you met a better player."

"You're not better… it was just luck," I croaked.

"Luck? What do you mean luck?"

"You drew four cards to complete a royal flush. The odds have to be thousands and thousands to one against that."

"Oh, no, you're wrong. The odds are more like a million to one, but luck played no part."

"Of course it was luck. You're the luckiest person in the world."

"I am blessed with the most wonderful wife in the world, exceptional children and grandchildren and relatively good health, but, as I said, luck is not a part of this equation."

"If it wasn't luck, then what was it?"

"I cheated," he said quietly.

"You what!"

"I cheated."

I was too stunned to even think of what words to say next.

"But of course I had help. Mrs. McCauley-Brown!" he yelled.

One of the double doors off to the side, the one that had been closed, slowly swung open to reveal Mrs. McCauley-Brown. It looked as though she'd pushed it open with her foot, and she offered a smile and a small wave. She was sitting at a small table, holding a telephone in one hand.

"My good friend is on the phone talking to Mr. Mc-Gregor. Turn around and look out the window."

I swivelled in my seat, and the bright sun caused me to shield my eyes.

"Do you see Mr. McGregor?"

I squinted and looked hard. I detected some motion and then saw him waving from the doorway of a small shed about a dozen yards away. He was holding something in one hand.

"Mr. McGregor has been reading your cards. Sometimes he'd practically come right to the window, and other times he'd use that powerful telescope, which allowed him to see your cards easily from where he is now standing. Then, using a telephone in the shed," he paused, "a most useful invention, the telephone—he called to Mrs. McCauley-Brown, who used hand signals, those used by the deaf to communicate, to relay the information to me."

"You have a telephone in the shed?" I asked in astonishment.

"Not usually. I put it in this afternoon. I am handy with things like that, you know. And earlier in the day I'd placed a call to an old acquaintance of mine in Washington. He's what you might call a card expert, a professional gambler, and he was most helpful in explaining how to set up this escapade. Of course he said I'd still need one more person's assistance."

"Who was that?"

"You."

"Me!"

"Yes, you. Without your help none of this would have been possible."

"I didn't help you!" I protested.

"Of course you did, starting with your choice of seats.

If you hadn't chosen that chair, with your back to the window, we couldn't have seen your cards. But I knew you'd sit there."

"How did you know?"

"It's an old trick of men conducting business, and a new trick of pilots fighting air battles, to always have the sun at their backs. I thought it might be a trick of poker players as well. And then I tried to give you a number of cues. Things like that little grimace when I didn't like the cards, always putting the bad cards on the left-hand side and betting more quickly when I had a frightfully bad hand. You did notice all of those, didn't you?"

"I noticed." What I didn't notice was being set up. "But it was still lucky that you got the royal flush."

"No. It was always right here," he said, tapping the money box. "I took those cards from an identical deck and simply put them in there before the game began. Then when I reached for the money, I grabbed those cards when I dumped the ones I didn't want. Here they are," he said, pulling them from the box. "Now does it all make sense to you?"

"Almost," I gasped, still overwhelmed with what he'd said, like it was all still an unbelievable nightmare. "I just don't understand why... why you went to all this trouble. The money can't mean that much to you. You're rich."

"Never too rich that a hundred dollars extra isn't welcome."

"But you can't keep the money. You cheated me!"

"Are you accusing Alexander Graham Bell of cheating?" he asked in a mocking tone. "Would anybody believe such an accusation, Mrs. McCauley-Brown?"

"Oh, no sir! You're known far and wide as a man of integrity."

"This isn't right... it isn't fair," I stammered.

"Cheating seldom is. Not here, not when you took money off the other employees with loaded dice, and not last night in town when you cheated those three young men."

"I didn't cheat any..." I started to say, but realized there was no point in even trying to argue.

"Of course you did, but let's not talk about what was. Instead let's discuss what will be." His voice was dark and deep and serious. "You must now work for me, for free, for the summer."

"But you cheated," I argued.

"Well, yes I did, but I cheated fair and square. Did you think it was right for Angus and his friends to try to beat you up?"

"Of course not, but this is different!"

"You're right. It is different, but not in the way you think. Cheating is cheating. It doesn't feel so good, does it? I want you to think about that sick feeling in your stomach when you lost and never forget it."

Remembering it would be simple because I didn't think it would ever leave my gut.

"And that sense of shock and outrage you feel right now, when you've discovered that somebody took unfair advantage of you simply to win a few dollars. And now I ask you, sir, will you keep your commitment, will you honour your word and agree to work here for the summer without pay?"

I didn't know what to say, and even if words came to

my head I didn't think I could force them through my clenched teeth. This was insane!

"Will you honour your commitment?" he demanded again.

Weakly I nodded my head.

"That is what I hoped. William, do you know why such efforts were taken tonight?"

To humiliate and cheat me, I thought, but remained silent.

"Because," he paused for a few seconds, which seemed to stretch out into forever, "because I like you and I am obligated to you."

"You cheated me because you like me?" I asked in astonishment.

"And because there is something worthwhile about you . . . something that is still there but will slip away unless it is saved. I am now going to present you with one more option."

Slowly and deliberately he took money from the pile in front of him and counted out one hundred and forty dollars. He pushed it toward me, leaving it on the table just in front of me.

"This is your wages for the entire summer as well as the money you took from the others. I want you to take it. You have two choices. You can keep all the money and leave, right now, go home or wherever it is you want to go. Or, you can return the money you won by cheating and remain here all summer and earn your wages. The choice is yours."

He got up and walked across the room, pausing at the door. "And by the way, if you decide to stay, your work assignment will be changed. You will be working exclusively under myself and Mr. Baldwin on the HD-4."

"The HD-4! You want me to work on the hydrofoil!" I exclaimed.

"Because of you the HD-4 is still here and not burnt to ashes. I believe you deserve the opportunity to work on it, but you must understand that you will spend much longer hours, and work much harder, on the hydrofoil than anyplace else on the estate. If you think you were working hard already, you have been mistaken. And as you've been told, there is an element of both importance and possible danger to being part of this enterprise. Now if you'll excuse me, I think my supper is getting cold. Please feel free to join us for dinner if you wish. I know Mrs. Bell would greatly enjoy your company... as would I."

He disappeared from the room leaving me alone. Mrs. McCauley-Brown had quietly slipped away from her post a moment before. The pile of money sat on the table before me. I picked it up and started to count it. Maybe this amount of money didn't mean anything to him, but it meant I could leave right now... if I wanted to. It was all up to me. I folded the money and stashed it in my pocket.

I still didn't know the layout of the house very well. Unless I left by the front door I'd have to pass by the dining room. The wooden floors were mostly covered by carpets and my feet made no sound as I moved. The doors to the dining room were open; I could hear conversation, and there was a burst of laughter. They were probably laughing at me. I peeked into the room. Mr.

and Mrs. Bell, Casey and four other guests were seated at the table. With the exception of Mr. Bell, who had just started eating, the rest were finishing up dessert.

"William, I'm glad you're going to join us!" Mrs. Bell said enthusiastically. "I'll have them warm up another plate!"

"No thanks, ma'am. I appreciate you inviting me and all, but I'm not going to eat with you tonight." My stomach was still far too upset to even consider eating. Almost certainly, anything that went in would come right back out.

"Perhaps another night," she said.

"Alec was telling me you've been offered an assignment working on the hydrofoil," Casey said.

I nodded.

"But William hasn't given me an answer yet," Bell added.

At that very moment, I really didn't have one to give.

"So, shall I expect to see you at the boathouse, bright and early tomorrow morning?" Mr. Bell asked.

"No."

"No?" he asked in a surprised tone. The look of disappointment on his face shocked me.

"No." I took a few steps and stopped, suddenly sure. "*You* won't see me in the morning. I'll be there, but you'll still be in bed until noon I'm sure."

I walked away on unsteady legs, and I heard the room behind me erupt into laughter.

Chapter Thirteen

I HURRIED DOWN THE noisy steps. It was almost seven o'clock and I wanted to get to the boathouse. I had a few chores Casey had given me the day before, my first day at the new job, and I wanted to finish them up before anybody else arrived. I was wondering if Mr. Bell would make another early appearance. I'd been shocked my first day working on the hydrofoil when I found him puttering around in the newly built boathouse. When Casey arrived about fifteen minutes later and saw Mr. Bell, he looked as though he was going to faint. Mr. Bell only stayed for an hour or so and then told us he had things to do elsewhere. Casey and I watched him walk away, and then Casey quietly said he was positive he was going back to bed and how grateful he was for that turn of events, since Mr. Bell could get very grumpy when he didn't have enough sleep.

Once I'd started working on the HD-4, Casey had explained to me why it was so important to keep the project confidential. The hydrofoil was being developed by Bell for the Royal Navy, and its purpose was to attack and destroy the Germans' U-boats, or submarines, which were proving to be so devastating to the navy's ships. If it worked, it would be a tremendously important weapon in the war effort.

Yesterday had been work, very hard work. Part of me still didn't believe that I'd chosen to stay here instead of just leaving with my money, but there was something about being there . . . it wasn't just shovelling sheep manure, we were doing something important. Whenever I wanted to sit down and take a break, I looked around and saw that everybody else was still working, so I kept working too.

They were continuing to change the angles on the foils that lifted the boat up off the water. Mostly I carted and fetched things, including bringing lunch down from the house, and cleaned up. I also used a brush to apply lacquer to waterproof the skin of the craft, and the fumes were terribly strong. They stung my eyes and left a terrible taste in my mouth, which didn't really go away completely until after I'd eaten my supper. We didn't leave until well past eight in the evening. They tried to chase me away earlier, but I refused to leave until the floor was so clean you could eat off it. Mrs. McCauley-Brown fixed me a big, late meal, which I ate in the kitchen while she told me stories about my mother as a schoolgirl. It sounded like she used to get into her share of trouble. Maybe she did know more about things in the world than I gave her credit for.

That morning I would double my pace. Casey was

going to take the boat out on the lake soon and told me if I finished up my work I might be able to come along for the ride. Although it was early and the sun was still low in the sky, it was already getting hot. It was going to be a scorching day, and it would be good to be on the water.

The big sliding door was partway open. It was left that way to let the fumes escape the building so there would be less chance of another fire. I took hold of the door and pushed it all the way open. The HD-4 was sitting on the rails in the middle of the building. It was really a strange contraption. The cockpit sat in a long thin tube that looked like a sixty-foot cigar with wings extending out on each side. The foils were like metal steps at the front and on both wings, and I was told the boat would rise up out of the water on the foils as it picked up speed.

Yesterday Casey had been tinkering with the engines and then started them up. Inside the building, the sound bounced back off the walls and was amazingly loud; so loud Casey gave me little pieces of rag to stuff in my ears.

"Good morning!" Casey beamed. He was taking sips from a steaming cup of coffee. In the other hand he was carrying a basket. "There's some more coffee in here," he said, "as well as sandwiches. You won't be able to go up to the house to get our lunch... unless you can walk on water."

A smile split my face.

"We'll put her in the water about eleven... assuming Alec is here by then."

"He's coming with us?"

"Not on the HD-4. He never goes on it, although Mrs. Bell has been out for a few rides. Alec will be accompanying us in a motor launch."

"Another boat will be coming along with us?"

"There's always a boat or two in escort. The observers can see things about the way the hydrofoil moves that can't be seen from the boat itself. Besides, it's a safety precaution."

"What do you mean?"

"It's just wise to have another boat in the water in case the HD-4 loses power or develops a leak... or crashes."

"Crashes!"

"Don't worry, nothing has ever happened, but it *is* an experimental boat."

I knew I could trust Casey, but that wouldn't stop me from worrying.

Just after noon we heard the rumble of a motor coming around the point and a motorboat appeared. Mr. Bell was sitting in a seat at the rear of the boat and Mr. McGregor was at the wheel. They came up close to the HD-4, where I was sitting up front with Casey, and yelled out greetings.

"It's a little choppy outside the shelter of the bay," Mr. Bell called out.

"It's important to test her in less than ideal circumstances. It's not like the Germans keep their U-boats in port when there's a bit of a blow."

"Regardless, I want you to take it slowly today. Nothing above fifty miles an hour. We want to test the angles on the foils, not set a new speed record," Mr. Bell warned loudly.

"Agreed!" Casey yelled back. He turned to me. "Here we go."

He pulled on a red lever, the ignition switch, and the twin engines sputtered and coughed and then came to life. The sound wasn't too bad. I guessed it was much quieter than yesterday in the boathouse because the sound wasn't bouncing back from the walls but was escaping across the open water.

"It's not too loud," I commented.

"I'm idling the engine. It will get a lot louder when I rev the motors, but in fact it'll seem quieter once we really get moving," Casey said. "We'll be travelling so fast we'll leave the sound behind us."

The HD-4 moved along behind the motor launch, keeping pace. We rounded the point and the waves hit us broadside and we bounced much more noticeably. It was rougher on the open water than in the shelter of the bay.

"Hold on," Casey warned. I felt the hydrofoil start to accelerate and I was pushed back against the seat.

As we picked up speed, the waves hitting the hull became louder and more frequent. We were taking a pounding and we still weren't moving that fast. I looked over my shoulder. Flickers of flame could be seen within the twin engines and between them I could see the motor launch being left farther behind. The engine became louder again as Casey gave it more gas. The pounding of the water became harder and spray started flying against and over the windscreen.

"How fast are we going?" I yelled.

"Maybe thirty miles an hour. It's too rough at this speed. I'm going to give it more power."

Before I could even think about what he'd said, I felt

the boat gain momentum, and we rose higher out of the water. At the same instant the pounding of the waves decreased dramatically and I realized we were no longer plowing through the water but skipping across the top. We were up on the hydrofoils, skimming along the top of the water! It was incredible! There was a sudden sensation of sideways movement. Casey was turning the HD-4. We were travelling in a large, smooth circle, and dead ahead, through the windscreen, I could see the motor launch.

"Ever driven a car before?" Casey asked.

"No, but I've seen it done. It doesn't look too hard."

"It isn't, and driving this isn't much different. You're just along for the ride today, but watch carefully. I'll let you drive a little on another run."

"Are you kidding?"

"I never kid about fun," Casey laughed.

"How fast are we going, anyway?"

"We're up to close to forty-five miles an hour. I'm going to slow it down a bit," Casey said.

"Couldn't we go just a little bit faster?"

Casey laughed out loud. "A man after my own heart. Not this time, but you can be with me when we open it up all the way."

"Promise?"

"Promise," he said with a smile. "But let's work on what we need to do today. I'm going to put the boat into a series of tight curves and turns. We'll circle the motor launch so they can observe the way it rides and responds."

I held on tightly as Casey swung the boat around.

There was a strange sensation as the boat responded to the turn by slipping sideways, like it was sliding along ice, throwing up a sheet of spray before it shot off forward again. Casey let out a laugh and I couldn't help but smile myself. It was incredible to be here, riding along.

Then I was struck by a sudden realization of what we were doing: we weren't simply out for a ride in a boat, we were experimenting with something that would be used to destroy German U-boats; something that would save the lives of sailors; something that could save the life of my father.

"Time to slow her down," Casey said. The engines throttled back and we slowed and started settling back into the water. "I told you there was nothing to worry about!"

I opened my mouth to answer when suddenly the world tilted over to the side and I felt myself being thrown through the air and then... nothing.

Chapter Fourteen

I COUGHED AND SPUTTERED and tried to sit up
but was held down by strong hands.

"What happened?" I asked as I looked around. I
was in the main house, and nearly a dozen people,
including Mr. and Mrs. Bell and Mrs. McCauley-
Brown, hovered over top of me.

"You're okay, dear, thank the good Lord you're
okay," Mrs. Bell exclaimed.

"But—"

She put her hand to my lips. "Shhh! Just lie still
while the doctor continues to examine you."

"I'm pretty well finished the exam," a man said.
"Except for that nasty bump on his head I can see
no other injuries. It's hard to tell with a head injury,
though. Let him sit up."

The hands released me and I pushed myself
up to a sitting position. I brought a hand up to my

forehead, which was throbbing. I recoiled in shock as I touched my head and pain shot through my entire body. There was an enormous bump, so large I could even make out the edge of the swelling when I looked up.

"Do you remember what happened?" the doctor asked.

"I was... I was out... in the HD-4... and... and then... where's Casey? Is he all right?" I asked desperately. I tried to look all around but my head got woozy and I thought I was going to throw up.

"He's all right," Mr. Bell said. "I think he has a broken arm."

"I haven't been able to examine him, though," the doctor added. "He wouldn't allow me to look at it until he was assured you were okay."

"Am I? Am I okay?"

"You have a terrible bump on your head, and your brain has been bruised, but I'm certain you'll be fine."

"I still don't know... what happened?"

"I'm afraid it's all my fault," Mr. Bell said. "Somehow I miscalculated the force and pressure on the foils... one of them snapped. I was certain, completely certain I had everything figured correctly, but obviously I was wrong, and my mistake sent you catapulting into the water. You must have hit your head against the boat, knocking you unconscious."

"We got you out of the water quickly. Casey had an arm around your neck, holding you above water when we got there. You'd been knocked out but you were breathing fine."

"And the HD-4, is it fine?"

"I didn't have an opportunity to assess the damage.

Whatever damage was done will be fixed. I am more concerned about you," Mr. Bell said sternly.

"I'm fine. The doctor said I'm fine."

"That's not what he said," Mrs. Bell corrected. "Mrs. McCauley-Brown, could you please make arrangements for William's things to be brought up to the main house and put in the guest room closest to my room."

"But I'm okay," I protested. I tried to rise to my feet, felt dizzy and had to sit back down.

"You're not okay. You must be observed, woken up every few hours. Isn't that correct, doctor?" she asked.

"Yes, it's a wise precaution."

"So I'll have no more debate about this. I'm bringing you up right now!"

She took me by the arm and helped guide me to my feet.

All at once Casey burst into the room. His left arm was in a sling and in his other hand he carried a piece of broken metal. It looked like one of the foils.

"Alec, you have to see this!" he practically yelled.

"Leave it alone now, Casey. There'll be time enough to look after the craft later, but for now we have to care for William and you."

"No! No, you don't understand! You have to look at this!"

"Casey, please put down the foil and . . ." Mr. Bell stopped and his face took on a look of complete confusion. "How did you get that foil, Casey? It would have dropped to the bottom of the lake when it broke off."

"This isn't the one that broke off on the water. This is the other front foil. We brought the HD-4 back up to the boathouse and when I put some weight against it, it simply snapped off."

"Impossible! Impossible! Your weight couldn't cause a piece of tempered metal to break!"

"It would if it were sawed most of the way through," Casey explained.

There was a pause and everybody looked from person to person, and then all eyes focused back on Casey.

"I examined the broken foil. Three-quarters of the way was a straight cut and the last quarter was jagged where it had broken under the pressure. And look at this." Casey dug into his pocket and then held his hand over top of the table. A fine dust filtered down and settled onto the surface. Bell put a finger into the small pile.

"Filings... metal filings," Bell said. "Where did you get these?"

"Off the floor of the boathouse. And I know the floor was completely clean when we left last night. William had that floor spotless."

Mr. Bell took the piece of metal from Casey. He turned it over and looked at the broken end. He ran a finger along the edge.

"It was terrible enough when this was simply an accident. Now it is more than an accident. You're saying somebody deliberately sabotaged the hydrofoil and did so in a manner that would result in a crash that could injure—or kill—the occupants of the craft."

"It would have been easy. They could have crossed the grounds or even come in off the lake. Nobody would have seen them."

"Can this discussion wait?" the doctor interrupted. "I

need to see that arm. And why are you holding your side?"

"It's a little tender. It feels like the time I cracked a rib playing rugby."

"We need to—" Mr. Bell began.

"You need to listen to the doctor!" Mrs. Bell interrupted. "I'm taking William to bed and you're going to allow the doctor to examine Casey!"

On unsteady feet I rose. My stomach churned, my legs buckled and I doubled over, throwing up all over the expensive carpet.

Chapter Fifteen

"BILLY!"

"Hi, Simon."

"It is so good to see you!" he exclaimed. "And you are fine? Yes?"

"I feel okay." I didn't want to admit that I still felt slightly light-headed. I'd had to tell Mrs. Bell I was feeling "perfect" before she'd even let me come downstairs to eat breakfast. Getting her to allow me out of the house was even harder.

"I was so worried… everybody on the whole staff was worried about you."

I laughed. "I'm sure old Isaac lost sleep over it."

"Maybe not Isaac, but many did." He paused. "If only I had insisted that you stay working in the orchard. I spoke to Mr. Bell and told him you were a good worker and I would welcome you back. Will you come back to work with me now?"

"Mr. Bell told me you were asking about me. Thanks for putting in a good word for me... but I want to stay where I am."

He reached out a hand and placed it on my shoulder. "I understand, but Billy, you be careful."

"I'm always careful. I have to get up to the boathouse. I'll see you later," I said.

"Yes, later."

I started to walk away.

"Billy, will you be coming back to live at the staff house soon?" Simon called out.

"I hope so, but it's not up to me. Mrs. Bell says I can't leave until *she* says I'm okay."

I waved goodbye again and started back toward the boathouse.

It felt good to be outside and moving around. For the last three days I'd been trapped inside the house. The first day it didn't matter. All I did was sleep, or want to sleep. By the second day I was anxious to get moving and nobody would let me. Between Mrs. Bell and Mrs. McCauley-Brown, I was hardly allowed to feed myself! Everybody had been so worried. At least that part had been okay... to have people caring about what happened to me.

At first Mrs. Bell had wanted my mother called, but I'd insisted that she not do it. There was no point in worrying her when there was nothing she could do. I told her I'd write my mother a letter and tell her that I was all right. It took some convincing, but she agreed. But when I tried to write the letter the day after the accident, I couldn't even focus on the paper and had to stop. I had to admit that even I was worried about me then.

It was good to see the boathouse. It was time to get back to work.

"William, it's wonderful to see you!" Casey yelled. He dropped his tools and came over to me. His left arm was encased in plaster.

"How are you feeling today?" he asked.

"Better today. Good enough to convince Mrs. Bell and Mrs. McCauley-Brown I could come out here."

Casey laughed. "They are a formidable pair. They tried to have me stop working because of my arm."

"Is it any better?" I asked.

"It's a bit of a pain… but not in the arm," he laughed. "I can still use it," he said, wiggling his fingers, "although it has slowed me down a bit. I'll be glad for your extra two good hands."

"How about the ribs?"

"No problem as long as I don't get into any footraces or breathe too deeply."

"And the HD-4?" I asked, looking it up and down.

"The replacement foils are being made in the machine shop and will be ready to be fitted by tomorrow, or the next day, at the latest. The damage to the hull was minimal and easily repaired. Maybe there were some benefits to the crash."

"What do you mean?"

"We thought the hull was tough and the accident proved it."

"No," I said firmly.

"No? What do you mean, no? Just look at how little damage was done."

"I'm not talking about that. What I mean is that it wasn't an accident."

"I guess that was a bad choice of words. I know there was nothing accidental about it. Alec has taken measures to make sure no more incidents will take place."

"What sort of measures?" I asked.

"Each night two men, armed with rifles, are posted outside the boathouse, which is sealed and locked."

"I guess the guards are good, but aren't you worried about the place being sealed up and another fire being started by spontaneous combustion?"

"I'm not worried about that at all, especially with the materials being stored in the shed. And I really never believed the fire was caused that way to begin with. Spontaneous combustion is what's blamed when nothing else can be found. Besides, we'd been using those same materials for weeks without problems."

"Is Mr. Bell taking any other measures?" I questioned.

"He's asked every single employee on the estate to stop and question any strangers they see. There are always so many guests around the place that I think we've all become too complacent and not observant enough."

"That won't help," I said quietly.

Casey gave me a questioning look. "Go on, please."

"It's just that I've been thinking a lot the last few days. Lying around in bed I haven't had anything to do but think. And I don't think any of this was done by a—"

"Stranger," Casey said, completing my sentence.

I nodded.

"I think you're right. Come here, I want to show you something." He walked over to the hydrofoil and stopped at one of the broken foils.

"This cut was made from the back to the front. Can you see, it's a smooth cut here, and then jagged metal here where it broke off?"

"Yes."

"Do you know what this means?"

I shook my head.

"When we were accelerating, going faster and faster, the pressure of our movement stopped the foil from breaking. It only broke when I cut back on the throttle and the gap opened up until it snapped."

"So?"

"So, if I had wanted to destroy the craft, really destroy it, I would have made the cuts from the other side to cause the foil to snap when we were going the fastest. Do you understand?"

"Yes," I nodded. "But maybe the person wasn't as smart as you and didn't know how to make the cuts."

"No, it was done in a very clever way, at just the right place. I think they cut it that way because they didn't want to kill the occupants."

"They didn't? They didn't miss by much," I said.

"Yes, but the probabilities of serious injury or death increase as the speed increases. If the collapse had occurred when we were going faster, the potential impact on us would have been more severe. Now do you understand?"

"I think so."

"And the other thing was, how did they know we were going out for a test ride the next day? Did you mention it to anybody?"

A rush of fear washed over me. Of course I'd mentioned it to some of the other men and Mrs. McCauley-Brown, and there was no telling who they'd told.

"I know I wasn't keeping it a secret," Casey continued. "I must have told a few people."

I felt relieved. He wasn't blaming me, and maybe it wasn't my fault.

"You know what they say, if you tell a secret to even one person, it is no longer a secret." Casey paused. "But Mr. Bell will hear none of this."

"He thinks this is an accident?" I asked in amazement.

"Oh no, of course not! What I mean is, he doesn't believe any of his staff could possibly be responsible."

"Have you explained everything? Told him your reasons?"

"I did, a few times, but he didn't believe me, or more likely didn't want to believe me. You have to understand that for Alec, we're not his employees, we're like his family. And he can't bring himself to think any member of his family would try to bring harm to any other member. For Alec, honour, integrity and loyalty are as much a part of life as food, drink and breath. He trusts us all. That's why he felt so badly keeping you away from the hydrofoil at first."

"He did?"

Casey nodded. "He saw your interest that first day and almost offered you the opportunity to work with us."

I didn't know what to say.

"I just wish he would take what I've said more seriously," Casey said.

"But there must be some way to convince him!"

"No, I'm afraid there isn't and…" Casey stopped and his brow furrowed. "You still haven't told me why *you* believed it wasn't done by a stranger."

I swallowed hard. "I guess because of the cuts and everything."

"But you thought it was an employee before I said a word. What aren't you telling me?"

I'd needed to tell somebody about the meeting in the arbour since that first night, but I didn't know who to trust or how to explain why I was out there in the first place. I looked at Casey. If there was one person I could trust, it was him. I took a deep breath and in one uninterrupted burst let the entire story drain out. Then I waited for his response.

"Something was happening, but it's hard to know exactly what it was. And you didn't see their faces?"

"Just feet. Shiny boots on one and dirty canvas work shoes on the other. I've looked for them. Mr. McGregor has a pair of riding boots that look a little the same, but not nearly as new or shiny. The only pair I've seen that looked anything like them were in town, worn by Corporal O'Malley."

"You can't think it was O'Malley!"

"No, of course not. I just meant they looked like his boots."

"Ah… like military boots."

"I guess so."

"And the shoes?" Casey questioned.

"Even worse. A lot of people have them… at Sheep-ville, in the orchard and on the farm. Do you know any-body who can speak another language around here?"

"Oh, lots of people. I can speak French," Casey answered.

"It wasn't French, but I don't know what it was. It sounded, I don't know, kind of *hard*."

"Hard… hmm… Gaelic always seems hard to me, and many of the people around Baddeck, a lot of employees, are Scottish and speak it."

"Isn't Isaac Scottish?" I asked.

"Originally… but there's no way it would be him. He's one stubborn old bird but as loyal as a hunting dog, and honest, too. It would have to be somebody else."

I was grateful Casey hadn't asked me what I was doing out there that night. He knew, and I knew he knew, I was doing something I shouldn't have been doing.

"Have you told anybody about this?"

"Just you. I didn't really know what it was about, just that they were doing something mysterious. It wasn't until I was lying in bed the past two days that I started to really wonder. Maybe we should talk to Mr. Bell," I sug-gested hesitantly. It was risky—maybe he'd ask why I was out there and realize you can't trust all the people who work for you.

"I think this has to stay between you and me, William."

I felt both relieved and worried at the same time. Somehow I thought if we involved Mr. Bell he could find a solution. Now it was up to me to help discover the answers.

"We must remain vigilant and discuss things we see or

hear, no matter how small. Perhaps we can put the little things together and find an answer. From this moment forward, William, you are the only one I will trust with my suspicions."

Casey reached out his good hand and we shook.

Chapter Sixteen

"WRITING TO YOUR MOTHER?"

I swivelled in my seat, away from the writing desk, to face Casey. "How did you know?"

"Mrs. Bell still makes *me* write to *my* mother every week. She says all the mothers in the world have to work together to make sure their children don't forget to write to them."

"She really does like writing and getting letters. You'd think with her husband inventing the telephone and all she'd just call people," I commented.

"She can't very well use the phone herself, now can she?" Casey said.

"Why can't she…" I let the sentence trail off as I remembered. She read lips so well, and she always seemed to know everything going on around her, that I kept forgetting she was deaf.

Casey smiled. "It's rare enough to see Alec using

the phone. If you ever want to see him angered, be there when somebody dares call during the dinner hour! I've heard him say a hundred times, 'Telephones are for calling out, not calling in,'" he said, sounding just like Mr. Bell.

I'd heard him say that myself.

"And with Mrs. Bell, letter-writing is an art. She enjoys putting words to paper. Her letters are more like beautiful stories or poems. I love when she writes me. You'll see what I mean in the fall. You can expect at least one or two letters from her during the winter months.

Casey closed the door noiselessly. He lifted up a chair and carried it over beside me. He put it down and sat on it backwards, straddling it to face me. "I've got some news."

I put the pen down on the side of the desk.

"I've been working on finding out who speaks different languages. There are quite a few, who either live here or in town."

"I think it's somebody who lives here," I said.

"Why do you think that?"

"If that meeting I overheard in the arbour was related, then the person definitely lives here. If at least one of them didn't, they could have met elsewhere, maybe even in town."

"That makes perfect sense." Casey beamed. "You're quite the police inspector! But I had to get the information on everybody who worked here or I couldn't have found out about anybody."

"What do you mean?"

"I had to ask Alec. The only other people who might know, like Mr. McGregor, might be suspects."

"You don't think Mr. McGregor or Mr. Stewart are responsible do you?" I asked in amazement.

"No, not really. I'd trust the two of them with my life. But the first rule is to trust no one… except for you and me."

"How did you ask Mr. Bell without him wanting to know why you were interested?"

"I told him I wanted to know so we could set up a list of employees who could act as guides and translators when our allies from all over the world want to see a demonstration of the hydrofoil," Casey said smugly.

"That's… that's brilliant!" I congratulated him.

"Mr. Bell thought so too… but of course for different reasons. As I thought, there are many staff who do speak Gaelic, three are fluent in French, half a dozen speak Dutch, almost all the gardeners are from Holland, three speak German—"

"German?"

"Yes," he said, nodding his head. "And I was thinking the same thing you were. What if they are really German spies?"

"Yes, spies."

"It's unlikely, though. Two were born and raised in Canada. The third is sixty-eight years old and has trouble getting around—he's got a bad leg—so he couldn't possibly be the man you heard. Alec almost didn't tell me about the German-speakers. He asked if I was planning on giving tours to the enemy."

"So I guess we're nowhere."

"Not nowhere, but nowhere near where I'd like us to be. I do have an idea, though. I think it would be good for you to move back to the staff house."

"I already suggested that to Mrs. Bell. She said I had to stay for at least one full week before she'd even consider allowing me to leave."

"Well, that's only two more days. I think you'd be better able to nose around, talk to the men, put a glass to the walls and listen and such," Casey suggested.

I chuckled. "You make it sound like a spy novel."

"Well, it is, isn't it?"

All at once the door burst open and Mrs. McCauley-Brown rushed in. Her expression was filled with fear. "There you are, Casey. I sent somebody out looking for you. There's a fire! A big fire!"

"Oh, my good Lord, not the boathouse!" Casey bounded to his feet.

"No, no, not the boathouse. It's up by Sheepville. It could be the barn or even the pens. You have to stop Mr. Bell. You know how he loves those sheep, and he might go and do something foolish! It was bad enough him going in after that fool boat of yours!"

"Where is Alec?" Casey demanded, rushing past Mrs. McCauley-Brown as she held the door.

"He's already gone!"

"Gone? Why did you let him go?" Casey demanded.

"Do you think I could have stopped him, even if I had a gun? Now quit wasting time and get after him!"

Casey rushed out of the room and I jumped up and hurried after him. He raced down the stairs and pushed through the side door, and I bounded down the steps right behind. We turned the side of the house and could clearly see dark smoke staining the night sky. Casey picked up the pace, but I noticed he was already breathing hard and was holding his broken arm against his injured ribs. I could tell by his face he was feeling pain with each breath.

"We have to slow down, it's too far to go at this speed!" I yelled.

He nodded in agreement and dropped the pace down to a trot.

"I thought for sure it was the boathouse too when I heard there was a fire," I said.

Casey didn't answer.

"But I guess we got lucky. There's not even any chance of it spreading to the boathouse. You can't get any farther away from the boathouse than Sheepville."

Casey and I both skidded to a stop at the same instant as the words I'd just spoken sank in.

"Do you think it's possible?" I asked to his unspoken question.

"I don't know. But if I was going to do something at the boathouse I'd create a diversion somewhere else. We've got to get to the boathouse right away!"

"But what about Mr. Bell? Would he really go into the fire after the sheep?"

"He might. Those sheep mean so much. He's been experimenting with them for years. He's close to developing a breed that gives birth only to twins. It would benefit people all over the world. Oh, William, we're caught. We can't be in two places at once."

"Why not, there are two of us?"

"The last time you didn't stop him from going into the burning building, you just crawled in after him, and I'm sure not sending you to the boathouse alone. We'll send somebody from the barn. Come on, we have to double our pace!"

Casey started moving. I hesitated and he pulled away a half dozen paces in front of me. Then, without stopping to think, I turned and started to run as fast as I could toward the boathouse. Within a few seconds Casey had noticed I wasn't with him and called out after me. I didn't even turn around to look. His voice faded away as I ran as fast as my legs would carry me. I broke through the outskirts of the forest.

At first I followed a fairly open path, but I had to cut off through the trees to take the fastest and most direct route. Despite the branches and trees that blocked the way I tried to keep my pace up. Then a branch caught me on the top of my head and I staggered slightly and had to slow my pace dramatically.

It was probably best anyway—what good would it do if I was completely exhausted when I arrived? I knew it wasn't too far and I'd soon be there and then ... and then what? I had no idea what or who was going to be there and what, if anything, I could do about it. After all, if a couple of men with guns couldn't defend it, what could I do?

The forest ended and I came out into the meadow. The outline of the boathouse was visible against the darkness of the water. There was no movement; all was quiet and still. I was hit with a sense of relief. I took a couple of deep breaths and slowed to a walk. I was wrong and everything was fine and... where were the guards? They were nowhere to be seen. Maybe they were just around the other side, by the sliding doors, and out of my sight. I moved slightly off to the side so I could see around the side without having to get too close. I moved slowly. It was dark, and I knew I was almost invisible. The soft pad of my feet against the grass was easily covered by the sounds of the waves breaking against the shore.

I looked up and down along the shore and couldn't see any indication of a boat. I continued forward. I could now see the front. There was nobody there, but it looked like the door was open a crack. Maybe they were inside. Slowly, putting one foot slightly in front of the other, I closed the distance. I stopped at the corner of the building and listened. Nothing. Then a beam of light flashed out the open door, skipped across the lake and vanished. If it was the guards, why would they be in there in the first place, and why would they use a flashlight instead of turning on the lights? I was certain that whoever was in this building was responsible... for whatever had happened to the guards. A shudder ran up my spine.

What was I supposed to do? I pressed myself against the building and tried to think. If only this had been a poker game I'd have known what to do. When you don't know what your opponent is holding but you know you have nothing, you either fold or bluff. Folding was easy; I could just run. Maybe I needed to bluff. But first I had to try to sneak a peek at the other guy's hand.

I circled around to the back of the building. There was a small window, big enough to vent fumes but not big enough for anybody to climb through. I eased up to the window and looked in. At first, I saw nothing, and then the beam of light swept across the building. I couldn't make out the figure holding the flashlight, but as far as I could see in the darkness there was only the one person. Whatever he was doing, he was doing it close to the hydrofoil.

I'd taken as much of a look as I could at the other guy's hand. Now—should I fold or bluff? There was only one choice.

I bent down and searched the ground. I found a large rock, and then a second and a third. I stood up, pulled back my arm and threw the largest of the rocks at the window. It hit the glass with a resounding smash. I shifted one of the two remaining rocks to my throwing hand and used it to bang against the side of the building. There was a scream of surprise from inside the boathouse. I sprinted a dozen feet and flung myself into the bushes. I was desperate for air but I didn't dare take a breath. I heard the sound of feet hitting gravel, and then it faded away. Whoever it was, he was gone! I felt safe, hidden in the bushes, surrounded by darkness. I could just lie here until Casey arrived. Unless of course the villain had already done his business before he left. Maybe there was a fire already burning, so small I couldn't see it yet, so small I could put it out before it became too large... but if I lay in the bushes it would just grow and grow and... I got up. I'd come too far to not go the rest of the way.

I walked quickly around the side of the building. I still clutched a rock in each hand and I squeezed the one in my right hand tightly. David only had one rock when he met Goliath. I had two. I was sure I'd heard feet running away… right? The door was still open and on the ground rested the lock to the boathouse. I bent down, dropped one of the rocks and picked up the lock, which had been snapped in two, probably by a pair of powerful bolt-cutters. I dropped the lock back to the ground.

Turning toward the entrance to the boathouse, the interior showed as a deeper dark. I leaned in and felt around with my hand until I found a switch. I flicked it, and the entire building was drenched in light. Terrified, I scanned the room. Nobody was there, and nothing seemed out of place. The HD-4 slept peacefully. I looked back over my shoulder, into the night, took a deep breath and stepped into the building.

Everything looked just as we'd left it when we'd locked up earlier that evening. I must have surprised him before he'd had a chance to do what he'd planned. I thought I should look at the hydrofoil more closely. I climbed up the ladder and peered into the cockpit. It looked fine. I jumped back down and moved over to the foils. Had he cut them again? I ran my hand up and down along the edges. I didn't feel anything and it looked fine. I took a rock and tapped it against the metal. It echoed back in a solid metallic tone. Just to be completely sure, I bent down to see if there was any trace of filings on the floor. I swept my hand along the floor; there was nothing, not even dust. Then I saw something, partially hidden by the rails, right in the middle of the tracks, directly under the HD-4.

I crawled underneath. Strips of torn up newspaper

were lying in a pile. He had been going to start another
fire! I reached out and grabbed at the shredded paper. As
I moved it I saw there were other objects, about the size
and shape of cigars, buried underneath. I picked one up
and brought it close. What was it?

The roar of a truck engine came rumbling through the
door and I straightened up and bashed my head on the
bottom of the hydrofoil.

"Ouch!" I screamed.

I crawled out from under the HD-4. My one hand still
held the strange object while I rubbed my head with the
other. I ran for the door and got there in time to see the
truck squeal to a stop. Mr. Bell, Casey and half a dozen
men, including the two guards, climbed out of the doors
or jumped off the back. I was awfully happy to see them
and gave a big wave.

"Are you all right, William? Is everything all right?"
Mr. Bell asked anxiously.

"Yeah, there was somebody here, but I chased him
away. Unfortunately I didn't see who it was. It sounded
like he ran off that way," I said, pointing down to the
lake.

Mr. Bell turned to the two guards, standing there holding their rifles. "It's probably too late, but go after him
anyway." They vanished into the darkness.

"What happened to them?" I asked.

"They saw the flames and went to investigate," Mr.
Bell said.

"Investigate," Casey scoffed. "They were curious and
wanted to have a look."

"Don't be too hard on them," Mr. Bell cautioned. "They were doing the best they could and... William... I want you to stay very calm."

"Calm? Of course I'm calm. Why wouldn't I be calm now?"

"I don't want anybody to argue with me or even question my words. I want everybody to back away from where William and I are standing," Mr. Bell said quietly.

With expressions that matched my confusion, the men, with the exception of Casey, backed off, leaving us in a large semicircle.

"You too, Casey," Mr. Bell said.

"Sorry, Alec, I can't do that. I think I know what William's holding, too."

"Holding? What am I holding?" I asked, looking at the object.

"Carefully, William, hold it carefully!" Mr. Bell paused. "I'm not certain but I believe it is an explosive."

"Explosive!" I hissed, holding it away from myself.

"Yes. Now I want you to give me your other hand and we're going to take a little walk."

"A walk," I echoed vacantly.

He took my hand and I followed along like a balloon on the end of a string. He led me straight for the water. Did he want me to toss it into the lake? To my surprise Mr. Bell stepped into the water.

"What are you doing?' I gasped.

"Don't talk, just walk with me," he said quietly.

I took a step into the shallows and a shiver ran up my leg. Mr. Bell led me into deeper water. A wave washed up over my knees. We continued to move. I shuddered as it slopped over my waist.

"Okay, William, lower your arm into the water and just let the charge go. Once it hits the water it'll be neutralized, even if it has a detonating cap."

I did as I was ordered, immersed my arm in the cold water, uncurled my fingers and released the stick of explosive.

Chapter Seventeen

I TURNED AND TWISTED and struggled to find a comfortable position to sleep in. The room was like an oven and I was bathed in sweat. The last few days had been hot. A couple of the locals, people who'd lived in Baddeck all their lives, said they couldn't ever remember it getting this hot. And there was no escape from the heat.

Working in the boathouse was even worse than being in my bedroom. The sun beat down on the metal roof all day, and when we left for the evening it would be sealed up as tight as a drum, trapping the hot air inside. In the morning, when the guards opened the door, the hot air would rush out.

Since the last attempt to destroy the HD-4 and the discovery of the explosives, a special kind of explosive more powerful than the army's dynamite, the guarding of the craft had been taken over by the

military. In shifts of six, unsmiling, serious, scowling soldiers stood on all sides of the boathouse. They'd turned
the building into a bunker, surrounding it with sandbag
walls that reached almost as high as my head. It should
have made me feel safer to be surrounded by a circle of
soldiers and sand, but instead I just felt more uneasy. It
was now impossible to forget, even for a second, what
had happened. And that was what was keeping me
awake that night, as much as the heat.

Along with the soldiers, the police had been around
the estate a lot over the last couple of weeks. They had
started interviewing all the employees, but Mr. Bell
threatened to throw them right off his property. He said
he'd rather burn the HD-4 himself than have anybody
falsely accuse his staff of wrongdoing. Corporal O'Malley
did not take any of this too kindly. He didn't strike me as
the sort of person who was accustomed to being told no.

A thread of cooler air tickled my face. The curtain
swayed ever so gently. I rolled off the bed and went to
the window, hoping I could somehow coax in, or capture,
another waft of wind. The window was open as far as it
could go, propped in place with a piece of two-by-four.
I'd even removed the screen because I didn't want anything to interfere with air coming in. I wasn't worried
about bugs; they seemed to be too hot to fly. Unfortunately, the vines growing up the trellis blocked off a little
bit of the space. I pushed some leaves back and peered
out past the main house to the water. Out at the view
that the Bells shared with me.

I thought about how nice and cool the water would
be... how nice it would feel to submerge my body in it

and just let every pore drink up the cool . . . but I was soon startled out of my reverie. Out on the water, a green light flashed three times rapidly. It was strange to think somebody might be fishing or travelling at this time of night. And if it were a boat, it would leave the lights on as running lights, not switch them on and off like that. Who knows? It could have been a lot of things, including my imagination.

Casey had accused me of letting my thoughts get carried away, although he was a fine one to talk! We'd continued to discuss our belief that the acts of sabotage were being undertaken by somebody here at the estate. I'd listened in on conversations, followed behind people and even tried putting a glass to the wall. All I'd found out was how stupid you feel when you put a glass against your . . . The three green flashes appeared again! This time there was no mistaking them. It seemed clear what they were: a signal. Somebody out on the water was trying to signal somebody else. Maybe somebody here on shore. Who were they signalling, and what were they trying to say? I knew the HD-4 was safe. The unsmiling soldiers would be standing guard all through the night until the next shift arrived at eight in the morning. The lights called once again! There seemed to be a pattern. About once a minute they were flashing.

On bare feet I padded almost silently across the floor. There was enough light to make out my pants and shirt draped over the chair. I'd stripped down to just my underwear to escape the heat when I was writing my mother a letter before bedtime. I was always careful to leave out all the stories about the dangerous things that had happened. Now, I couldn't help but compose a letter in my head that would explain everything.

Dear Mom,

I'm okay. So far I've almost been beaten up, I've run into a burning building and was almost burned to a crisp, I've chased away a spy and I've held enough explosives to blow a crater in the ground as big as a house. I'm doing just fine and hope you and Sis are too. I have to stop writing now because I'm watching a mysterious signal that I think has something to do with the spy.

All my love,
William

I chuckled to myself, thinking about her reaction to my imaginary letter, and what my father would think when he finally arrived home and saw it. I'd been sent up here because it was supposed to be safer than being in the city. And everybody was so worried that my father was risking his life at sea! Maybe someday, a long, long time from now, I'd tell them about all the things that had really happened.

I grabbed my shoes and hurried back to the window, arriving just in time to see another series of signals. Whoever it was, was pretty persistent. I slipped on my pants and shirt and then tied up my shoes. I didn't know for what, but I did want to be ready.

It was hard to focus on the blackness of the water, but at least it was slightly cooler by the window, and an occasional wisp of a breeze was my reward. The light continued to call out, and I started to count between signals—every sixty seconds. A couple of times I felt overwhelmed by sleep and my head nodded down for an instant, or possibly more, before I woke up again. It was important to keep watching. Something was happening or going to happen... at least I thought it was.

The lights flashed again: green, red, green... green, red, green! Something had changed. I counted out the seconds until the next signal was scheduled. I reached sixty and kept on counting. There was nothing. Maybe I was counting too fast, or maybe I'd closed my eyes for just a second and during the blink the lights had escaped my detection. I kept counting, straining my eyes to make out anything out there on the darkened lake. No matter how hard I stared, I couldn't squeeze more lights out of the darkness. Whatever had happened was over. I should just go to bed.

Then I heard the sound. Somebody was trying to move silently down the stairs. The steps answered back noisily. I rose and readied myself to run to the door, fling it open and finally see who was responsible. I took one step and froze; seeing who it was would prove nothing. They could just say they were going out for a walk, or a smoke, unable to sleep, like me, because of the heat.

I turned back to the window and leaned out to try to make out the door at the bottom. I knew I'd be invisible buried beneath the leaves and surrounded by the night. I saw the door, and a glint of thin, weak moonlight bounced off the glass as it opened. There was not nearly enough light to make out who it was, but I could see him cast his gaze all around, like he was checking to see if he was being watched. There were twenty-one of us living in the staff house now. At one point I'd suspected every-one—whether they lived here or away—but there was never anything to any of it. But now... who could it be? He started slowly across the meadow. I had to follow.

My thoughts turned to the door and then the stairs beyond. It would be just as impossible for me to get down without them groaning out a warning, a warning that could be heard throughout the building. What if he had an accomplice still in the building, or the sound leaked out into the still night air?

What about the trellis? After the fires on the property I'd checked it out carefully to see if it could support me. It wasn't very strong, but it seemed secure enough to use in the event of an emergency, and this was an emergency.

I reached out and took hold of it. I shook it once—it seemed solidly anchored—and then climbed out. The thick foliage engulfed me and I was well hidden and felt safe. I reached with my left foot for the next foothold, stepped down and repeated the same procedure again and again until I stepped down onto the ground.

Anxiously I looked all around. No one had seen me, but now that I was out I realized there was no way I could still see the person who'd left before me. He'd dis-appeared into the darkness. I could stumble after him in the rough direction he'd headed, but there was no guar-antee I'd find him, or that he wouldn't hear or see me coming first.

I had to think. Maybe I could wake up Casey and he'd help me... but help me do what, exactly? His room was on the third floor and there was no way to get him with-out risking waking the whole house. I didn't want to even attempt to explain any of this to Mr. Bell. Shoot! None of this mattered anyway. I'd forgotten, Casey had left this evening for Truro. He had to pick up some new equipment and wouldn't be back until late tomorrow or the next day. Maybe there was another way. You didn't need to follow somebody if you knew where they were going.

I started running across the meadow in a slightly different direction than that taken by the man. If I was right, I knew his destination, and he'd taken a longer route to avoid being seen by anybody. I didn't care if I was seen, except by him and whoever he was going to meet. All I cared about was getting there before either he or the other man arrived, and taking up my position.

I pushed my back against the blocks lining the back of the bench in the arbour and made sure my feet and knees were well out of sight, hidden by the seat. I didn't think I had anything to worry about; the shadows cast by the overhanging branches of the trees and bushes were even darker than the night sky. The blocks and ground felt cold right through my shirt and a shiver ran up my spine. I wasn't sure if it had anything to do with the cold, though.

There was no chance now of falling asleep. I felt more awake than I ever remembered being. I was still trying to control my breath. I was winded from my run, but I couldn't afford to have anybody hear me panting. I rubbed my right cheek. It was stinging badly from where I'd run headlong into a branch. I couldn't worry about that. I had two more important things to worry about: that they weren't going to meet here... and that they were. I wasn't sure which I feared more.

I heard a sound… again… maybe. This was the fourth time I'd thought I'd heard something. Each time it had only been my imagination, or maybe a small animal out looking for its supper. At least I didn't have to worry about Bruno the bear any more. The sound was getting louder. Too loud to be coming from inside my head. Somebody was coming along the path. I pictured polished leather boots against the gravel. Then there was a whistle and my head jerked up in surprise, almost hitting the bottom of the seat. Within a few seconds an answering call came from the other direction and I knew which fear I was about to face: they were going to meet here again.

Within seconds of the second whistle I heard another set of footsteps coming toward me along the path. Louder and louder, closer and closer, until first one set of feet, the moonlight reflecting off the polished boots, and then the second pair stood directly in front of me. The two men began to talk. I could hear them, although they spoke in whispers, but couldn't understand the words. Once again they were speaking a foreign language. I didn't know for sure, but I thought it was German. That was just my mind playing tricks with me, though, because I didn't even really know what German sounded like.

They sat down on the bench. I allowed myself a silent smile. I knew I was invisible underneath their perch. Unfortunately if they couldn't see me I couldn't see them either, and I needed to know who they were. I perked my ears, hoping I would recognize the voice even if it was speaking a language I didn't understand.

As they continued to talk they seemed to be getting louder, and the tone became more tense, almost angry. Suddenly the man in the canvas shoes leapt to his feet.

"Why do you want to know that?" a voice called out in English. The voice was so familiar.

The answer was still in the foreign language.

"Just answer my question! Why do you want to know where Mr. Bell's bedroom is located?" he demanded.

I don't know what shocked me more, the question, or the realization that I did know the voice. It was Simon! He was one of the last people in the world I would have suspected.

The second voice responded again, and while the language was still foreign, the tone was unmistakable: anger.

"I need you to answer my question first. Why do you want to know where Mr. Bell's room is located?" Simon asked in a loud voice.

My God! What were they planning on doing?

"Be quiet!" the other man hissed back in a clipped English. He stood up, and now the two men stood directly in front of me. "Are you having a change of heart?"

"Please tell me," Simon pleaded.

The other man laughed and it sent a chill through my body. It was an evil sound.

"We need to know how to find Mr. Bell's room because you have failed us. You have failed to destroy the hydrofoil."

"I tried very hard, but—"

It was Simon all along! It was Simon who almost killed me!

"I do not wish to hear excuses. My superiors will not

accept excuses or failures and neither will I. I did not bring my men all the way across the Atlantic Ocean to fail."

His words struck me like a slap in the face. They were spies, and there were more than just one or two of them.

"Your bungling has caused them to put guards on the craft and it is now much more difficult to get to. That is why we must find an easier target. Now tell me, in what part of the mansion does Mr. Bell sleep?"

"You can't mean to harm him, can you?" Simon asked.

"It is of no concern to you."

"But I have known the man for years and—"

"And you did not hesitate when it came to taking our money to set those fires and betray him!"

"That was different!"

"Different, hah! You betrayed him for a few dollars and now you have developed a conscience. Traitors are traitors!"

"I am not a traitor! I was doing it for my country! My mother was German!" Simon protested.

"A loyal German does not ask for money. Your loyalty was to your wallet. Now, for the last time, where in the mansion does Mr. Bell sleep?"

There was a long pause. I held my breath and waited. Ever so slightly I shifted myself. I still couldn't see their faces but I could see almost all of their bodies.

"And if I don't tell you?" Simon asked.

"It makes our job only slightly more difficult. We will be going into the house tonight and finding him, with or without your help. And when we do…" He let the sentence fade away into silence.

"I won't let you!" Simon said loudly. "I'll alert the authorities!"

"The operation will be underway in a matter of minutes. No one can be summoned in time to save Mr. Bell. All you would be doing is signing your own death warrant. They hang spies and traitors, or didn't you know?" He laughed again. It was like this was just a game, and he seemed to be enjoying it.

"I do not believe you have the courage to go to the authorities. But I cannot take chances. Here is the final payment you so richly deserve!"

He leaped forward and the light flashed off something in his hand which streaked toward Simon. Simon cried out in pain and every hair on my body stood on end. He collapsed in a pile onto the gravel right in front of my face, so close a cloud of dust swirled under the bench. I forced one of my hands over my mouth to stifle a gasp. Simon was lying on the ground, right in front of me, his head only a few inches from mine. He looked at me and his eyes widened in surprise. He'd seen me! His mouth curled in a smile, and a soft chuckle seemed to escape. Then his whole body shuddered, he took a deep breath, and he closed his eyes.

A shiny boot rolled him forward until he was partway under the bench. The man offered a few more words, words I couldn't understand, and then started walking away. I heard his footfalls recede down the path until I knew I was all alone. All alone except for Simon.

Chapter Eighteen

"SIMON," I CALLED OUT SOFTLY.

There was no answer. I didn't really expect there to be one.

"Simon…"

He didn't answer or move, and I strained my ears to try to hear breathing. There was nothing.

"Are you all right?" Of course he wasn't all right. The question was whether he was even alive. But somehow the sound of my voice seemed to calm me.

"I have to get up, so I'm going to have to squeeze by you."

The only thing less likely than Simon answering was me getting through the little space between him and the top of the bench.

"I'm just going to move you a little."

I put my hand against his chest and gently pushed

against him. He didn't budge. I drew up my other hand
and with both shoved him hard. He rolled over, freeing
me from the bench. As I drew myself up I realized my
hands were all sticky and... they were covered in blood!
His chest was covered in blood! I leaped backwards,
practically tripping over the bench, furiously rubbing my
hands against my shirt. Somehow his death seemed
much more awful now that I had seen, and felt, the
blood leaking out of his body. I felt a rush of nausea,
started to gag, doubled over and threw up into the
bushes behind the bench. Then I stumbled forward and
almost tripped over Simon. I gagged a second time,
heaved, but nothing came out. My head was reeling. I
had to sit down, but I couldn't do it there, with Simon
bleeding at my feet.

I staggered down the path, pushed out through some
bushes and collapsed on the grass of the meadow. The
grass, wet with the dew, felt cool and refreshing against
my head, and my stomach settled back down into my
body. I took a deep breath...and then another... and
then a third. I felt better with each breath. I sat up. I
knew I didn't have time to sit there any longer.

I had two choices: run to the boathouse and get the
soldiers to come back to the house with me to protect
Mr. Bell, or go to the house directly by myself and get
him and everybody out before the spies arrived. The
man in the boots had a head start on me, but I knew the
grounds, and even on shaky legs I was sure I could move
faster than him. As well, I figured he had to go and meet
up with the others who were probably waiting by the
shore in a boat.

My first impulse was to go to the boathouse and get the guards. But then I realized that even if I did tell them what was happening there was no guarantee they'd believe me or come with me to the house. They might just figure I was trying to make them abandon their post, the way the guards had before to see the fire at Sheepville, and they might refuse to go, or even worse, they might stop me from leaving. I couldn't take the chance. I stood up and set out for the main house.

I pushed open the back door. The whole house was sleeping in silent darkness. I felt my way around the kitchen. I couldn't turn on any lights. I didn't know how close they were, but even from a distance they'd be able to see the lights, and I couldn't risk it.

"Ouch!" I cried out as I stubbed my toe on something. I grabbed my foot and hopped around the room.

A light flashed on and I brought my hands quickly up to my face to block my eyes.

"William, what are you doing in here in the middle of the night? Couldn't you wait until morning to get a snack?" Mrs. McCauley-Brown asked as she stood sleepily in the doorway. "And what is that all over your shirt?"

I lunged across the door and flicked the light switch off.

"William, what in the name of goodness—"

"We can't turn on the lights. You have to listen to me. There are men, I don't know how many, but they're going to come in here and do something to Mr. Bell!"

"William, slow down, slow down!"

"There isn't time! They're coming to get Mr. Bell!"

"Who's coming to get him?"

"Spies, German secret agents!"

"Oh, William, you must be dreaming! This is non-sense, now wake up and—"

I grabbed her by roughly by the collar of her night-gown. "This is no dream, it's a nightmare, and if we don't hurry nobody is going to wake up. Those stains on my shirt are blood... Simon's blood... he's dead, and Mr. Bell is next."

A strange gurgling sound came out of her mouth but no words.

"We have to get Mr. Bell, and everybody else, out of the house. How many people are here tonight?"

"Um... um..." she stammered.

"How many? How many?" I demanded.

"There's Mr. Bell and Mrs. Bell... and... Casey..."

"Casey's gone away!"

"Oh, yes, that's right. There's nobody else here tonight. Everybody's—"

Her words were stopped by the sound of a door being shoved open and feet hitting the wooden floor of the front hallway.

"Go around the back and get Mr. and Mrs. Bell and get them out through the window. I'll hold them off."

"But, how can you—"

"Never mind, just go," I whispered, and I pushed her toward the back way to the Bells' bedroom by the sun-room.

I heard thundering feet climbing the steps to the upstairs rooms. Then I saw a light come on under the door to the dining room. I had only seconds before they'd come into the room. After kicking off my shoes, I unbuttoned my blood-stained shirt, threw it down, and with my foot I pushed it under the table until it was hidden by the long tablecloth.

I grabbed the handle to the refrigerator and flung it open. I snatched a chicken leg and took a big bite just as the door to the kitchen was kicked in. A man dressed in black, holding a rifle, burst into the room. I stifled a scream and flung my hands up into the air.

"What do you want?" I yelled.

He ran across the room, his rifle leading the way, and shoved the barrel into my stomach.

"*Schnell, schnell!*" he yelled.

He grabbed me by the arm and I dropped the piece of chicken to the floor. He flung me toward the door to the dining room. I staggered, regained my balance and then was almost knocked down again as he thrust the barrel of the rifle into my back. A second man appeared, also dressed in black and carrying a rifle. He held the door open and I was pushed through the dining room and into the main entranceway. There were two men standing there, and I could hear others running around the house. I was gripped with fear, and the only thing keeping me together at all was the firm belief that none of this could be real. I closed my eyes and prayed the others had gotten away… and that I'd live to find out.

A hand gripped my face and my eyes popped open. I was staring into the eyes of a tall, imposing man standing only inches in front of me.

"Hello, William," he said, and I recognized the voice. He was the man from the arbour. The man who had killed Simon. He let go of my face. He was smiling. I looked down and saw his boots. They weren't as shiny as before. They were covered with dust from the path.

"You must be wondering how I know who you are," he told me.

I nodded my head. I was so afraid I didn't know if I could talk.

"I know many things. Many things indeed. You have caused me great trouble and inconvenience."

I wanted to say something, but my tongue felt so thick and swollen I didn't know if any words could be forced out of my throat.

Within thirty seconds a half dozen men showed up, coming from all different parts of the house. A few words were exchanged in German. There were now ten of them. It was clear that the man standing before me, the man who had killed Simon, was the leader.

He turned his attention back to me. "Where is Mr. Bell?" he demanded loudly.

"He's... he's not here... he's gone away for the night... nobody's here... but me," I stammered.

"Which room is his?" he yelled.

"It's at the . . . at the top of the stairs," I answered, directing him to the special guest room, the fanciest bedroom in the house.

He barked out a few words and two of the men ran up the stairs. They kicked in the door, but of course, reappeared almost instantly. They yelled something that I didn't understand.

He sneered and then withdrew a pistol from his holster. He raised it to my head.

"I do not believe you," he said quietly. "Tell me where he is or you shall die."

My head froze.

I heard the hammer of the gun cock. "Tell me now." He said the words softly, almost in a whisper. There was a wild look in his eyes, and I wondered if he wanted me to talk or just an excuse to kill me too.

"I... I told you... he's gone... they went away for the weekend... please believe me. Can't you tell his bed hasn't even been slept in?" I pleaded.

"Not been slept in?" He turned around and yelled out something.

"*Nein, nein,*" came the response from one of the men at the top of the steps.

He chuckled, the way he'd chuckled before sticking the knife into Simon. I wanted to yell out or run or fight or something, but I knew it was pointless. I was going to die, but at least I wouldn't die without a reason.

"Now I believe you. Few people lie with a gun to their heads. How old are you, William?"

"What?" I croaked.

"How old are you?"

"I'm fifteen."

"Fifteen? And in what month is your birthday? When do you become sixteen?" he asked in his stilted English.

"March, March the third."

"One of my favourite months. The winter is receding and the flowers are just starting to emerge. March is a beautiful month in Germany. I don't imagine you've ever been to Germany, have you, William?"

"No."

"Too many of your countrymen are trying to see more of Germany than we would like. You know, William, for all the trouble you have caused me, you deserve a bullet in the head."

With all my strength I fought the urge to call out or break into tears or crumple to the floor. Then, with the little bit of power left in my body, I raised my eyes from the ground and looked him square in the eyes. I wanted to see the man who was going to kill me.

"And if this was March the third instead of August, I would kill you. We Germans are civilized people. We do not kill innocent women and children." He removed his pistol from my head and held it at his side.

Without my realizing it, a snicker fell from my lips.

"Something I said was funny?" he asked. "Perhaps you do not think we are civilized. Do not believe all the things you read in the newspapers. We are not butchers of innocents."

"Unless they're aboard ships!" I suddenly blurted out. I couldn't understand where these words were coming from. I'd won the bluff, and my life with it, and now I was on the verge of throwing it all away.

"What did you say?" he asked angrily.

"Sneaking up on ships with submarines and killing innocent men and women and children with torpedoes! My father is a sailor!"

"Ah, so that is why this is so personal for you. Now I understand," he said, nodding his head.

"And I hope you understand that I was able to help

with the HD-4! Once it gets out there it'll blow your U-boats right out of the water!"

He snarled at me and then barked out an order. Instantly my arms were grabbed by two of the men.

"I do not know whether you are brave or a fool. But I do know one thing for certain. While we failed to get Bell, the hydrofoil will be destroyed, tonight, in the next few minutes."

"Hah!" I snapped. I knew my speech had cost me my life, so what did I have to lose? "The guards will cut you down the instant you try to get anywhere near the boathouse!"

"You are correct, and that is why we are not going to get close to the boathouse."

A chair was thrust under me and I was pushed down into in. Rope was coiled around my hands and legs. A gag was forced into my mouth and tied behind my head. I willingly accepted the ropes because I knew what it meant: I was going to be left to live. You don't tie up a dead man.

"Do you know much about submarines, William?"

I shook my head. Even if I'd tried, the gag would have prevented me from talking. I was almost grateful because being gagged would stop me from saying anything else to ignite his temper.

"I thought not. My submarine, yes, I am one of those cowardly submarine captains you speak of, has a cannon mounted on the front deck. When the craft surfaces, that gun is surprisingly accurate to a range of one mile. I will bring my boat to a point just off the shore of the boathouse and open fire. I will fire until all that remains is a crater where the hydrofoil now rests. I preferred a simpler approach, but now I am left with no choice. I will not fail in my mission."

He yelled out another order and all of the men filed out of the room, leaving just the two of us alone. He bent down close to my ear.

"You will live and probably have a very long life. What I want you to remember, remember always, is that it was *you* who failed. You failed to protect the hydrofoil and even more, you stood before a man who might very well be the captain of the vessel that will kill your father some day, and you were unable to stop him. You failed. Goodbye."

He tapped my cheek with his hand, smiled wickedly and then left the room, leaving me alone with my thoughts. Maybe I'd failed in some things, but I'd succeeded in keeping them from getting to Mr. Bell. Even if they destroyed the HD-4, we could always build another one, and...

My thoughts were cut off by a blood-curdling scream punctuated by rapid gunshots. I strained against the ropes and a cry tried to force its way past the gag. Had they got Mr. and Mrs. Bell and Mrs. McCauley-Brown? I surged forward, pushing my toes against the floor. The chair tipped and I toppled over, crashing heavily, face first into the floor. I heard rapid footfalls, like those made by military boots hitting the wooden floors, the sound of the door slamming and then nothing.

Chapter Nineteen

THOSE SCREAMS—THEY had to have come from the Bells and Mrs. McCauley-Brown! If they weren't already dead, they'd be bleeding to death, and I was helpless. I struggled and thrashed but the ropes held firm and dug painfully into my skin. I started to cry. They were the first tears I'd shed in a long time.

"William!" cried out a voice.

My eyes popped open. It was Mr. Bell! He was alive!

"William, where are you, lad? Where are you?" he screamed.

I called out, but my muffled voice didn't reach beyond the entranceway.

"William are you…?" Mr. Bell rushed in and saw me. "He's here, he's here!"

He grabbed the chair and effortlessly lifted it onto its feet. Mrs. Bell and Mrs. McCauley-Brown came running from two different directions. They both threw their arms around me.

"Ladies, give me some space so we can untie the lad." They backed away as he struggled with the gag.

"Mabel, go to the front door and make sure those men are still moving away. Mrs. McCauley-Brown, please go and telephone the authorities."

The two ladies leapt into action while Mr. Bell pulled the gag from my mouth. Small pieces of fibre stuck to my tongue.

"I thought you were dead... the gunshots," I stammered.

He quickly started to work on freeing my hands. "We thought it was you who was dead. I couldn't have lived with that. I never should have put you at risk. I wanted to come out of hiding and give myself up but the women convinced me to stay. They said to have faith... faith that you could play poker with them and bluff your way. And you did it, William, you did it! I need to untie you so I can shake your hand!"

Mrs. McCauley-Brown reappeared. "The telephone is dead!"

"The lines were probably cut. That would never happen with messages transmitted through a beam of light. I have to begin work on that immediately after—"

"We have to get to the HD-4!" I blurted out.

"Certainly they won't attack the fortifications, and even if they do, what good would the four of us be?" Mr. Bell asked.

"They're going to attack it from the water. They're going to use the cannon on the submarine."

"Submarine? They have a submarine! We have to get down there and warn the soldiers. Maybe they have some weaponry to fight against it!" Mr. Bell announced. "Mrs. McCauley-Brown, help free William's legs."

Mrs. Bell reappeared in the doorway. In her hands was a mass of black. At first I couldn't make it out, and then the shape came into focus. It was Bruno's head!

"I think the sounds you all heard were made by one of those men accidentally stumbling into Bruno. His head has been cut off by gunfire . . . the wall behind him is pocked with bullet holes."

I pictured that evil man bumping into Bruno and for just an instant feeling the same fear I'd felt that dark night when I'd first been "introduced" to the bear, that same fear I'd felt tonight facing him. I started snickering, and the snicker became a laugh, and the laugh grew until I felt tears of a different kind leaking out of the corners of my eyes. I hoped Bruno had scared him so good he'd wet *his* pants too, and the pee had run down into his shining boots!

"Are you all right, lad?" Mr. Bell asked in alarm.

I nodded. "We have to get going."

The car skidded and swerved along the path leading up to the boathouse. We'd narrowly missed a tree and flattened down some bushes as we hurtled down the narrow downhill stretch. The engine roared and the gears ground noisily as Mr. Bell worked to gather more speed. I'd never driven with him before, and I was beginning to think his driving was a greater threat to my life than anything I'd faced tonight. Of course, it didn't help that he was driving with the lights out to avoid alerting any observers on the lake.

"We can't help if we die in a car crash!" I yelled out.

"Hah! Don't be afraid of a little speed, William," he replied, turning to me.

"Look out!" I screamed as we veered slightly off the path and through a series of bushes. The decapitated tops bounced off the windscreen and over the top of the car before we hit the path again.

"Maybe I could ease up just a little," Mr. Bell said quietly.

The path levelled out and opened into the meadow. We crossed the opening in seconds and were there at the boathouse. Mr. Bell slammed on the brakes, sending the car in a side spin toward the building. I clutched the seat with both hands, hanging on for dear life. It looked as though we weren't going to drive *to* the boathouse, we were going *through* it! Maybe we'd save the Germans the work of destroying the HD-4 by doing it ourselves!

We came to a hard stop and were overtaken by a cloud of dust and dirt that swirled in through the open windows. Out the driver's side of the vehicle I could see what had stopped us—the sandbag barricade of the building! Just as I'd regained my senses, a rifle punched through the cloud of dust. They hadn't gone back to the submarine like he'd said! He'd tricked me, and now they were here and we were their prisoners! I'd led Mr. Bell into a trap!

I looked up from the point of the rifle, through the dust, and felt like crying out for joy. It was being held by one of our soldiers. Seeing us blaze down the road and ram the building must have scared them as much as they'd just scared me.

"Put down the rifle, man!" Mr. Bell bellowed.

"I'm sorry, Mr. Bell... we didn't know it was you," he apologized as he withdrew his gun from the window and opened the door. Mr. Bell pushed me out the door and followed after me because his door was blocked by the barricades.

"There's no time for talk. We need you to extinguish all lights and to remove the sandbags blocking the big door and ramp!" he yelled as he strode toward the entrance to the building.

"But sir, I can't do that! I'm under orders—"

"What you are going to be is under attack in a matter of minutes or less!"

"Under attack! Then shouldn't we man the barricade, not open up a wall? We must defend our post."

Mr. Bell pushed aside two men who were standing by the doorway. He reached into his pocket, fumbling for the key to the lock.

"You can't stop this attack, unless you have a battleship in your backpack."

"A battleship... I don't understand..."

"Of course you don't! Soon a submarine will appear in the water directly in front of this building and its cannon will rain down fire until it reduces this building and its contents to charred splinters. Do you have any defence against such an enemy?"

"Um... no... I guess we could fire our rifles, and maybe we could—"

"Maybe nothing. If you remain here, you and your men

will become part of the blackened contents of the building. Now get out of my way and all of you get to work
clearing the sandbags off of the railroad tracks. Now!"

The soldier snapped to attention and saluted, and he
and his men scrambled to the barrier.

"William, come in and help me with the HD-4," he
said as he pushed in through the door.

I followed but hesitated at the doorway. I pictured a
submarine, out on the water, invisible to our eyes, readying its cannon—a shot flying through the air, landing on
the boathouse, blowing us into a million tiny pieces.

"Come on, William, don't worry. We'll be given some
warning. The first shot will be off target and will be used
for them to correct aim for the next. There should be a
gap between shots, perhaps up to thirty seconds, while
they reload. It could very well take them a dozen tries to
hit the building."

Reassured, I rushed in after him and hurried to the
HD-4.

"Of course, I've heard the Germans have very accurate gunners, so perhaps they *can* hit us on the first try,"
he said very matter-of-factly.

I looked over at him and could see his eyes were alive
with laughter, despite the seriousness of his voice.

"Remove the blocks and then get the sliding door
open, while I—"

His words were obliterated by a deafening crash of
thunder and the sound of smashing glass. A shell had
fallen so close to the building that it had blown out the
back window. It was the same one they'd replaced after
I'd smashed it with the rock.

"Hurry!" Mr. Bell yelled as he started up the ladder to the cockpit of the craft.

I threw myself under the hydrofoil and grappled with the blocks. The first two came out easily but I had to struggle with the third, which was wedged in tightly. Slowly the HD-4 started to move.

"The door, William! The door!"

It was going to hit the still-closed door. I rolled to the side, barely missing one of the foils, bounded to my feet and caught the door. I flung it open with all my might and it slid out of the way just as the tail of the HD-4 was about to hit it.

Half a dozen feet farther away, four of the soldiers were removing the last of the sandbags blocking the ramp. The two others were by the water, and their rifles sounded as they shot at the submarine. I stared out at it, barely visible off shore.

There was a flash of light from the deck of the submarine and before I could even think what it meant a tremendous explosion ripped open the night. I looked up in time to see the hydrofoil rolling down the track toward the water. I scrambled to my knees and on all fours scuttled forward and grabbed hold of one of the foils. I was dragged along the ground as it picked up speed. I wasn't going to let it get away. It splashed into the lake and water sprayed up at me, hitting me in the face like a cold slap. Using the foil as a ladder I climbed up the side, pulling myself up, step by step, until I mounted the wing and then tumbled over into the cockpit.

"William, you shouldn't be here! It's too dangerous! Get over the side!" Bell was sitting behind the wheel.

"And what are *you* going to do?"

"I'm going to drive her to safety, of course… at least as soon as I can get her started… I can't tell in the dark… is it this switch?… or perhaps…"

I leaned forward and pulled the throttle out. The engines flashed with fire as the fuel ignited and they roared to life.

"You've never even been for a ride in it, let alone driven it!" I shouted over the engines.

"There's always a first time!"

"But not now. Let me drive! Casey lets me drive all the time!" I lied. He'd let me behind the wheel for one short ride.

"You're bluffing me, aren't you, William?"

Despite everything a small laugh escaped my lips. "Of course I am, but I still have more experience driving it than you do."

The steady barking of the soldiers' rifles was overwhelmed by an explosion and a *whoosh* and a shower of water washed over us! A shell had exploded just off the side of the ship and it rocked us wildly. Mr. Bell slid across the bench seat, freeing the space behind the wheel.

I plopped down, turned the wheel hard and gave it some throttle. The hydrofoil leaped forward and the shore disappeared as we circled out toward open water.

"Give it some more power, William! More power!"

The boat burst forward as though it had been stung by a hornet, and we were thrown backwards against our seats. At the same time I turned hard to port, away from the U-boat. Spray bounced off the windscreen and a series of pinging sounds punctuated the noise of the engines. The ride became smoother as we rose up onto the foils and out of the water.

"Circle it wide to this side and then head under full throttle to Baddeck. We have to escape and telephone the military so they can bottle off both exits to the sea! We can trap them!"

I looked back, saw another flash of light come from the submarine and braced myself for the explosion. I heard the shot soar over our heads and explode into the water just yards ahead of us. A funnel of water shot into the air and rained down on us, and once again we were rocked violently to the side.

"Open it up! We have to go faster!"

"I can't!" I yelled back.

"What do you mean, you can't? I know she can move faster than this."

"See the mark on the throttle? This is as fast as Casey has ever gone in the trials."

Bell reached over and grabbed the throttle. "The time for trials is over," he said, as he pulled it out and the engines roared louder and we rose farther out of the water.

"More speed!" he yelled. "Open it up all the way!"

I pulled the throttle out all the way and we rose up another notch. The ride was so smooth it was as though we'd slowed down instead of gained speed.

Another shot rang out and I braced for the impact.

"It hit well behind us," Bell said. "We're out of range!"

I reached for the throttle to slow us down, but Mr. Bell took my hand.

"Leave it wide until we hit the harbour. A few seconds might make all the difference."

We skimmed across the water until the lights of Baddeck appeared dead ahead. I throttled back and we rattled and rolled as we settled back into the water.

"Congratulations, William," Mr. Bell said.

"Congratulations, yourself."

"No, no, you don't understand. I took a mark on the coast and on my watch when you opened it to full throttle. We travelled one and a quarter miles in fifty-eight seconds. Our top speed was somewhere in excess of seventy miles per hour. Do you know what that means, William?"

I shrugged. "That we were travelling pretty fast, I guess."

"Pretty fast is an understatement. We were travelling faster than any men have ever travelled across water. We just set a world record! And you were the driver!"

Chapter Twenty

"HERE, YOU MIGHT WANT to see this," Mr. Bell said, slapping down a newspaper on the workbench in front of me.

I opened up the paper and looked at the front page. There was a picture of a submarine, run aground, with a gaping hole extending along the side. Underneath was a bold headline that read:

**SUB CAPTURED DUE TO BELL
AND YOUTHFUL HELPER!**

I didn't need to read the story as I'd already had it all explained to me. In trying to elude the navy ships that were pursuing it, the sub had run up onto a sandbar. The captain, rather than let his vessel be captured and investigated, ordered the crew to abandon ship and then set it on fire and set off explosives. The sub was just a gutted hulk. All twenty-three members of the crew were rescued and captured. The captain was believed to have perished in the fire and explosions, his body consumed by the flames.

"Oh, good Lord, you didn't bring him a paper, did you?" Casey called out from across the building. "It's bad enough he took away my chance to set a speed record, but now his head is going to get so big it won't fit through the door!" He crossed over and playfully ruffled my hair.

"I don't suppose you've written your mother to tell her about your adventures," Mr. Bell said.

"No, but I guess she'll find out about at least some of it now from the papers."

"Aye, she will. This is the Sydney paper, but I can't imagine this isn't news across the country and across the ocean to the other side."

"Do you want me to call her on the telephone?"

"Yes, you place the call, but then I want to personally extend an invitation," he said.

"An invitation to what?"

"For your parents and your sister to come to the estate for a visit."

"My father probably isn't even home. He could be on a boat anywhere between Halifax and England."

"Perhaps. If that is the case then perhaps they can come without your father. If your mother is anything like my dear mother, she'll need to lay eyes on you and throw her arms around you before she'll completely believe you're all right."

"That would be wonderful!" I gushed. I so wanted to see my mother and my sister and... my father. I did want to see him, as much as I wanted to see the rest of my family. Maybe I had things to say to him, and things I hoped he'd say to me. I guess I'd learned that everyone has to play the cards he's dealt and do the best with what he's got. If my father wasn't the man I wanted him to be, maybe it was up to me to find out why, to drop my poker face and let him know how I felt. I could only hope he'd meet me halfway.

"We'll prepare a room for them."

"There are two beds in my room."

"No, there's only one." He paused. "You realize I don't mean your room up in the staff house, but here at the house. That is now your permanent room."

"But I thought that was just for last night, after all the excitement and everything."

"Certainly not! All my special guests . . . and my family… stay in the main house, and that's where you'll be staying. If that's all right with you?"

I just smiled in response.

Casey laughed and put an arm around my shoulder.

"You and Casey have become quite a pair. And I guess you were right about things. What a sad tragedy… with Simon."

"It is sad, Alec," Casey agreed.

"I guess I can't always trust people to do the right thing," Mr. Bell said, shaking his head slowly.

"But he was *trying* to do the right thing," I disagreed.

"What do you mean, William?"

"In the end, when it really mattered, he was trying to do the right thing. He gave up his life trying to do the right thing."

Mr. Bell's eyes softened and a smile spread through his bushy beard. "You are right, William, it sounds as though he gave his life trying to do the right thing. I think it is better that his part in the sabotage never be known. Let his soul rest in peace."

I nodded in agreement.

"But enough talk of sad things. There's much work to be done on the HD-4, and I'd like to finish it before our junior helper has to return to Halifax in September to continue his schooling. If all goes as planned, perhaps you can make the return journey in the company of your family."

"I could stay if you still need my help," I protested.

"Not a possibility. Your schooling is important. An engineer needs to have a fine and formal education."

"An engineer?"

"Aye. Didn't I tell you that's what you're going to become?" he said with a lilt in his voice and laughter in his eyes. "Far better money than playing poker, although a man still has to have his mathematics, understand probability and know when to fold or play his cards. You do want to become an engineer, don't you?"

"I was sort of thinking about it," I answered.

"I hope you were more than 'sort of thinking about it'," Casey broke in. "I've already been on the phone to my old school, the University of Toronto. Two years from now, if you keep your marks up, they've reserved a spot for you."

"But—"

"No buts," Mr. Bell interrupted. "It's a good school, and an expensive one, too. You'll have to study hard and save all your money. I've already put aside your wages for next summer."

"Next summer?"

"Of course. Did you think I'd be letting you work any place else but here?"

The smile that split my face threatened to circle right around my head and meet in the back.

"By the way, William, have you ever flown in an airplane?"

"An airplane?"

He smiled. "Maybe I shouldn't get so far ahead of myself... let's take care of this project before we start working on the one for next summer."